MERCHANT TO THE LORDS OF DEATH

John J Swetnam

CHAPTER ONE

The procession that carried the body of Twin Jaguars along the causeway to the cluster of temples was far from the most lavish in the history of Tikal, the greatest of Maya cities. Just four years before when his mother, Jaguar Throne, had been laid to rest underneath the great staircase of the Temple of the Masks, five servants had broken through the circle of priests to demand that they be buried with her. The cries of the mourners, it was said, had echoed out across the plazas until they could be heard in the farthest house compounds. Twin Jaguars' bier was followed by only a slave woman and her seven year old daughter, chance captives from a Coban trading expedition, jostled along within the circle of priests, both looking decidedly unenthusiastic about their impending trip through the underworld. The murmur of the mourners as the body passed barely drowned out the cries of vendors from the marketplace in the far plaza.

"Scandalous, isn't it?" said a voice in 8 Manik's ear. The thought so closely paralleled his own that he started. It was as if a chac had been sent from the Alligator God to communicate with him. 8 Manik spun around to see a much younger man, leaning with an air of indolence and sarcasm, on the wall where the temple abutted the causeway.

"My lord..." 8 Manik began, for, although the young man wore a simple breechcloth without ornamentation, the piercing of his lower lip showed that he had often sacrificed blood in the temples and thus must enjoy special favor with the priesthood. The cloth he wore might look simple to some, but 8 Manik could see that it was woven of Mexican cotton, carried at great expense from the Tajin lands to the north.

"Scandalous, but not surprising," the man continued. "Tikal was once great, but that was long ago. Since our defeat by Caracol, we have endured a century of paying tribute instead of collecting it. Our most sacred stelas have been thrown down and left shattered for all to see. Shield Skull, our late lamented ruler, tried to establish our independence, was captured, and sacrificed. Now his son sickens and dies just months after his investiture. It will be as if his reign had never happened. I'll wager his successor eliminates him from the list of rulers."

"I am honored that you should choose to speak with me." 8 Manik began. The things this man was saying were true, but they were the kind of dangerous truths one does not speak openly.

The young man waved away the polite forms of deference before 8 Manik could continue. "Come with me, merchant," he said and turned away without even bothering to make the required obeisance toward the bier. This person must either be extremely powerful or foolishly brave, 8 Manik thought as he followed him away from the plaza. To turn one's back on a corpse was an act of such calculated rudeness that no one who saw it would fail to notice. Tikal might be the grandest city of those which spoke the Mayan tongue, but it was still small enough that people would note every action and talk about it. Anything that was talked about was reported, if not to the lords of the city, then certainly to the priests who were their relatives and allies. Bad luck followed those who failed to show reverence, and whether because the gods called them or because some human agent killed them, they were unlikely to see the next turn of the sacred year.

The arrogant stranger did not look back as he cut across the corner of the plaza and headed up the causeway that led to the north. The two giant pyramids, which flanked the plaza, stood on an enormous artificial platform that the citizens of the city had raised, it was said, two baktuns (calendrical cycles of 260 years each) ago. The elevated roadways which linked the center to enormous structures to the southeast, west, and north were designed to permit travelers and processions alike to move with ease among the sacred shines and monumental palaces which dominated the city. In between these thoroughfares, thatched huts and family compounds created a crazy quilt maze, baffling to strangers but well known to everyone in the city. 8 Manik saw that the stranger was headed not to the perimeter of the city, but to the area next to the central reservoir .

The young man turned into a jumble of houses that led down a slope toward the west. 8 Manik knew the area only by reputation. The makers of Tikal's distinctive pottery had their homes and workshops there, and he traded only feathers and cacao beans. He jostled against these men in the marketplace, wedging his way down the narrow aisles that separated the stalls of the women who dominated the trade of the city, but his business took him to the far-off cities of Mexico. Members of the trading guilds looked down upon the potters, who worked with their hands and whose business seldom took them away from the city overnight.

The house compounds of the potters looked poor to 8 Manik's practiced eye, with gaps in the cornstalk walls and roof thatching that was only half as thick as necessary to ward off the torrential downpours of the rainy season. The children in the paths that wound between the compounds were listless, with bowed legs and thin hair. Many were bloated with the sickness of the poor. Some of these families never ate meat, and even the black beans the traders ate every day were probably too expensive for a potter's family more than twice in the twenty days that made up each month.

The young man swiftly turned into a doorway no larger than the rest. 8 Manik, following the imperious youth through the narrow gate in the front wall and into the courtyard, came up short. A young woman of incredible beauty, naked to the waist, was kneeling on the beaten dirt floor of the patio with her forehead to the ground. She had placed the foot of the young man on her neck. A baby as fat and well fed as the children in the street had been emaciated clung to her skirt, looking up at the man with large, frightened eyes.

"Greet our guests," the young man ordered, removing his foot. "Find us some food. Funerals make me hungry."

To 8 Manik's intense embarrassment, the woman began to crawl across the ground toward him, reaching for his ankle. It made him angry to see a Mayan woman treated in this way. A slave or the women from the highlands in the north might be expected to display such extravagant deference, but the women of the jungle cities were famous for their strength and independence. There was a scar on 8

Manik's left arm from a brawl that started when a drunken trader from Monte Alban had made a slighting remark about the women of Tikal being nothing but men with breasts. No one could let such an insult to his natal city pass unanswered, and 8 Manik wore his scar with pride.

"Get up," he hissed, "Act like a woman of Tikal!"

"Bring us some food right away," repeated the young lord, and the woman bustled to the rear of the compound, dragging her son with her. The noble stepped into the room next to the gateway to the street, motioning for 8 Manik to follow him. Inside, the packed earth floor was covered with woven textiles of enormous value. With a graceful, practiced motion the lord sat cross-legged. Ashamed at standing with his head higher than that of his better, 8 Manik quickly sat as well.

The two of them stared at each other, each trying to judge the other's character. 8 Manik saw before him a young man of aristocratic demeanor but whom he had never seen in any of the great public spectacles of the city. He was brutally handsome with the aristocratic sloping forehead, down-turned nose and drooping lower lip that the Mayans prized as beautiful. The long black hair was pulled back away from his face, accentuating the grace of his features. He was taller than the average man, slender and strong, not with the burly muscularity of a peasant but with the grace of one who has spent his hours practicing to play in the ball court rituals or hunting in the jungles to the east.

I wonder what he sees when he looks at me, 8 Manik thought. A merchant who has climbed the high passes and traveled along the Avenue of the

Dead in the great, ruined metropolis of Teotihucan? A wily trader who has amassed enough profit to endow both his sons with expeditions of their own? A man who has given his only daughter to a peasant along with enough land to support both of them? He knew who I was and sought me out, so he must know that much at least.

This compound might look like a potter's dwelling from the outside, but the wealth of the interior was stunning. At one end of the room was a low wooden platform, such as those on which the lord of the city might sit cross-legged while receiving embassies from other Maya cities. Everywhere in the weaving reappeared the figure of the god with the tripartite headdress. Only one man in the city, the kalomte, the Sun Lord, the all-powerful ruler to whom the cahals or lower lords acknowledged fealty, wore this symbol.

"8 Manik," the young Lord began in an almost trancelike tone. "A name of singular fortune, the day of all which is most prized both for its potential for growth and its certainty of wealth. Your mother must have been proud to have borne you on such a day."

"She had no time to be proud, my Lord," said 8 Manik. "I was born in a torrent of blood, and she lived, I am told, long enough to hold me to her breast but once."

"The chacs carry cactus whips to beat the rain from the clouds. Often they chastise those whom they intend to raise on high."

"A humble trader such as I would never be worthy of a chac's attention," 8 Manik parried, "They say 'The gods reserve both their blessings and their wrath for those who sacrifice to them.'"

"So the old maxims say," responded the lord, "but I believe that the gods have a special interest in the common man. The Sacred Twins themselves who entered the world of the Dead and defeated the Lords of the underworld were born to an ordinary woman."

Such palaver could go on all day, thought 8 Manik. "Surely, my lord," he said, "You did not summon me for enlightenment on philosophy or religion. Would it be too forward to ask what I am doing here?"

"A bold assertion," said the young man who did not look displeased. From the far side of the compound came the rhythmic slapping of the woman patting out tortillas before toasting them on a hot clay griddle. "And quite correct," he continued, "I did not bring you here to discuss philosophy. It is the way with those of us who do not dirty our hands with labor to introduce each conversation with a little commentary on religion. But I could not expect you to know that."

8 Manik wondered whether this man was incredibly rude or so innocent of the ways of the world that he didn't realize just how condescending his words were. Either way, 8 Manik knew that someone so vain and thoughtless could only get him into trouble. "Perhaps my Lord would be interested in sponsoring a trading journey," he said, trying to look stupid. The great families of Tikal never spoke of wealth or status, but they were not above financing a trading venture by "giving" a trader the means to purchase a stock of goods. Such sponsorship was repaid along with a "gift" of half the profits of the expedition.

"I brought you here," the Lord continued, abandoning his abstract tone, "to save Tikal."

"Every man of Tikal stands ready to give his life for his city," said 8 Manik, hiding in patriotic clichés. "I have stood in battle many times and am only too willing to fall in battle if need be."

"If it were only matter of winning a battle," said the young lord, leaning forward and staring at 8 Manik intently, "I could easily raise an army. I have been trained as a warrior and a king. What I need from you is your knowledge."

"I am a humble merchant," 8 Manik protested.

"And you will do as I say!" the young man flashed in anger. "If I needed warriors, I would not go among merchants to find my men. I need a man who can help me overcome a plot to destroy the ruling family. I need someone who is clever and who can move about unseen. But most of all, I need a man favored by the gods."

The young man's grand phrases frightened 8 Manik, but they also annoyed him. He had been born, it was true, on a lucky day. The date 8 Manik recurred every 260 days of the sacred round of days, and every 52 years it occurred on the same day of the solar year. But to be born on 8 Manik was hardly unique. There were probably two hundred men in Tikal who shared his date of birth. Besides, to refer to a person's individual fate was a liberty only taken by one's closest associates. This young lord, however well connected, had no right to command him to follow. The man might be crazy, or merely irresponsible. 8 Manik shared with all the Maya a love of order. Impulsive men were like children and should be treated as such. In a calculated affront, he rose to his feet.

"My Lord," he said, "I do not know your name or your age, though I suspect I have a son who is older than you are. If he spoke in my presence as you do now, I would take a limb of the nearest tree and beat him. And even though he is the father of a child of his own, he would accept my reproof as proper and would not raise a hand to shield himself from my blows!"

A slow smile crept across the face with the arrogant features. "A son of Jaguar Throne, the great lady of Tikal, beaten by a commoner. This city has existed for a thousand years, and it has never seen such an event."

"Jaguar Throne's only son is dead," said 8 Manik. "We witnessed his burial this very day. We must await his rebirth in a new ruler, as the royal house renews itself."

"You believe that drivel?" snapped the young lord." The spirit of the dead lord descends to the underworld, only to reemerge as a later ruler?"

"It is not for me to say," muttered 8 Manik. Was this man trying to draw him into heresy? This must be some sort of trap, designed by the priests, to ferret out those who wished to harm the royal family. First this young man publicly turns his back on the corpse of a dead ruler, brings him here to this house where the customs are foreign, then he claims to be an heir to the throne. This young man would not live long if he acted with such reckless abandon.

"This is growing boring," the young man answered. "I have brought you here for a purpose. It was my intention to grace you with the honor of eating a meal with me, but I'm not sure that you deserve such accolades. I am told that you are the most resourceful of the merchants, so I have chosen you to do my bidding. If you do not agree, your sons need never fear your parental wrath again."

8 Manik stared at the younger man, his heart pounding against his chest. It was true that he had a reputation as a canny trader as well as an industrious one. He had not inherited a stock of trading goods, as many in his guild had, but had labored long to accumulate the wealth necessary to provide his daughter a dowry and his sons with inventories of their own. He was used to bargaining with men who were his equals, and, while he had been bested in some transactions and cheated in a few, he was confident of his abilities to judge both men and goods and take care of himself in the long run.

Now he felt as if he were lost in a forest. If this man were a son of Jaguar Throne, insane as that seemed, then 8 Manik knew he could carry out his threat. "The lords sacrifice their blood for Tikal," the old saying went, "but they drink its blood as well." Taken in its most innocent sense, the saying referred not only to the blood sacrifices expected of noble leaders who symbolically fertilized the soil during rituals by thrusting cactus spines through their lips, ear lobes, and even their foreskins, to water the earth. They also led the men of Tikal into battles from which many would not return. The second meaning of the saying was that the lords preyed upon the commoner class, drinking the blood of the lower classes by arranging the deaths of those who would oppose them. 8 Manik knew that a true noble would not hesitate to avenge what he saw as a challenge to his authority.

But how could this man be the son of Jaguar Throne? Every birth or death in the ruling lineage had been publicly announced since Stormy Sky had founded the royal line two dozen generations ago. The servants and wet nurses who attended the noble wives loved to tell stories of their charges. The telling and retelling of each small detail made their names great to those around them. When Twin Jaguars, as a seven-year-old child, had fallen and broken one of his teeth on his first trip into the sacred precinct in the Temple of the Masks, the news had spread to the furthest neighborhoods within the hour. For the next twenty years, when he spoke in public, people strained to see the crooked tooth in his mouth and nudged each other when he smiled. There could not possibly be a child of the royal family unknown to everyone in Tikal.

"Why do you think our late ruler was named Twin Jaguars?" asked the lord, breaking the silence that had flooded the room as 8 Manik stopped to think.

"A most auspicious name," the merchant replied, "Twinning always brings good fortune, like the Hero Twins who broke the power of the lords of death in the great ball game they played in the underworld of Xibalba. Jaguar means power, mastery, destruction. The founder of his lineage was named Jaguar Skull. Good fortune and great power, what better name for a ruler?"

"A pretty story," said the young man, "but sit down and I will tell you a prettier one. One that happens to be true, as well."

Reluctantly 8 Manik lowered himself to the floor again. He realized that he could not escape this conversation without offending someone of great wealth and perhaps great power. The best course of action would be to politely hear this man out and find a way to slip away. He had friends and contacts among half the cities of the Maya world. To flee Tikal might mean the loss of his wealth, but he could preserve the lives of his wife and his children and start again. The traders guild loved to tell the fable of the merchant who drowned crossing the river because he insisted on holding on to his stock. Wealth came and went, the story pointed out, but the successful trader was one who accepted the blows of fate and survived to keep on trading

"Twin Jaguars was born at the start of the rainy season," the young man began. He had turned his face away from 8 Manik and stared into the rafters above him, almost as if he could see through the thatch and into the sky beyond. "His birth was nearly a month earlier than expected. His mother, Jaguar Throne, had not begun the period of sequestration that is normal for a woman of her rank in which she abandons the outside world to focus all her energies on the development of the new life within. She was, in fact, returning from Uaxactun where she had been visiting her mother's sister, the wife of that lord that barely acknowledges our dominion."

As he spoke, the young noble's voice assumed the singsong quality of one who is telling a tale which is to be repeated over and over again. The words flowed smoothly, one image following its predecessor. His voice reminded 8 Manik of the words of a priest, recounting one of the myths which explained where the world had come from, the multiple destructions it had endured, and the eventual, and temporary, emergence of the world of the present.

"Knowing that labor is a dangerous time, her steward arranged for a runner to be sent to Tikal to bring a litter so that Jaguar Throne could be carried to the city. Since she could not walk upon her journey, she was assisted to a hut that farmers build so that they can rest overnight during the height of the harvest season. Jaguar Throne entered the house to rest and found within a woman, also in labor, a girl little older than twelve, who was stifling the groans of her contractions in a desperate attempt to keep her presence silent. The rest of Jaguar Throne's party remained outside, fearful of contaminating the sacred space that must attend the creation of a noble child.

"Three children were born in that hut, three children born within one hour. One was the child of a peasant girl who had been molested by a traveler, a life which, once made, was gone without having drawn a breath. The sons of Jaguar Throne both lived. One returned with Jaguar Throne to be acknowledged as heir to the throne of Tikal. The second she sent to her homeland, Palenque, to be nursed by that same young girl and raised by Jaguar Throne's father's family in that far land. The one child she named Twin Jaguars. The second she named Twin Rabbit.

"Rabbit is also a name of good fortune," hazarded 8 Manik. "If Rabbit had not deceived the lords of the underworld by imitating the ball which escaped from the ball court, then the Hero Twins could never have overcome them."

"You follow my point quickly," said the young noble, "Jaguar Throne knew that to bring two equal heirs to Tikal might disrupt the lineage which Shield Skull was attempting to restore. From great trouble comes great happiness, but happiness can never last in this world."

"I never speak of these things," 8 Manik interjected. No one in Tikal dared speak of the disastrous defeat three generations before in which Caracol had imposed its rule on the city. Through generations of scheming and raiding, the ruling lineage had gradually begun to assert its independence. Shield Skull had been the first to openly defy the established order, but he had been captured, and eventually sacrificed, by the lord of Dos Pilas, the close ally of Caracol. It had taken two years for Tikal to negotiate the return and burial of his remains.

"She knew," the lord continued, ignoring as was only proper, 8 Manik's patriotic interruption, "that just as my father, Shield Skull, was the reincarnation of Stormy Sky, so too the line of Stormy Sky had difficulty taking root and was followed by trouble. She saw the birth of twins as divine intervention to save Tikal from dynastic troubles fated to follow so great a leader as my father. She sent me, like a rabbit, to deflect the forces of death, for she knew that in the end I would return to ensure the unbroken line of rulership. It is I who shall rule Tikal, guarding it like a father and ensuring its greatness."

The young lord had become more and more animated as he spoke, and his voice rang out in the room as if he were shouting to a plaza full of people. Now he sprang to his feet and began pacing back and forth.

"He's crazy," 8 Manik said to himself. "Perhaps someone has done magic to make him take leave of his senses. A man like this will not survive long, and everyone who is near him is liable to be tainted by his reputation, if not suffer his fate."

"You doubt me?" cried Twin Rabbit. "Then explain how it is that I carry this?"

He reached into a small pouch that hung at his hip and produced a magnificent jade knife and held it aloft. "This is the sacrificial knife which Stormy Sky used when he conducted the sacrifices which established our lineage. My mother sent this with me as a token of my royalty. Who else could carry the most sacred object of the royal house but the one she meant to rule?"

8 Manik stared at the blade in the noble's hand and wondered if it were really the royal knife. It was certainly a magnificent piece of work, but he had no way of knowing its authenticity. Common people had heard of such fabulous and magically powerful heirlooms, but they would never get close enough during the great rituals to see the knife as it was wielded.

A deferential cough from the doorway interrupted the tirade. The young woman stood there, holding a steaming basket of tamales. Their odor filled the room. She had made the traditional Mayan tamale, large and soft, wrapped in the broad green leaves of the forest, tied like a package with a strip of bark, and wrapped in a second leaf whose sole purpose was to augment the aroma of the meal. As a traveler to the highlands in the north, 8 Manik knew of the smaller, harder tamales wrapped in cornhusks, and like any good Mayan, regarded them as unworthy of notice.

"Food," exclaimed Twin Rabbit, "You may eat with me after all, merchant. I despise the habit of eating alone."

The young woman cringed into the room, holding the basket before her. He snatched the basket from her and selected the largest tamale for himself, then pushed the remainder toward 8 Manik. The merchant appreciated the good form the young man was exhibiting. To offer the basket to him first would have forced him to run the risk of choosing the tamale his superior preferred. This way he knew he need not worry about giving offense.

Twin Rabbit sat and quickly unwrapped the neat parcel before him. The odor of tomatoes, chilies, turkey, epizote, and highland oregano filled the room. This was food which men like 8 Manik ate only on special occasions, such as weddings or funerals. Fish from the drainage canals was the best flesh that most artisans could hope for. 8 Manik opened his tamale, carefully mimicking the actions of his superior.

"Eat well," the young lord ordered. "You and I have a great journey to undertake. Before it is done, we will have traveled to Palenque and back. Soon I will stand atop the Temple of the Masks and be given the clothing which only the gods will wear -- the apron of the Maize god, the headdress of the Celestial Bird, the double serpent staff which holds up the sky. My footprints in blood will be outlined on the sacred paper that carpets my route up the steps of the temple. I will stand before the multitude as god and king, and I will present them with the greatest tribute which a city could ever receive -- the heart of the Lord Pakal, ruler of Palenque!"

8 Manik knew that those who are insane must not be startled, but he could not help flinching when he heard these words. The lord Pakal was a man uniquely favored by fortune. He had built what had been a minor center into a major power of the Mayan World. To strike at such a man was to strike at the gods themselves, for it was they who had placed him on his throne. If the story Twin Rabbit had told was true, he was proposing to kill his own grandfather, for Pakal was the father of Jaguar Throne, the lady of Tikal and the mother of its dead lord, Twin Jaguar, who was even now

being laid in his crypt. Was there no limit to the man's impiety?

"Eat now as I eat!" commanded Twin Rabbit. He dipped his fingers into the cooling tamale and raised it to his lips.

Reluctantly 8 Manik followed his orders. The tamale's rich savory taste on his tongue was strange and wonderful, but he couldn't enjoy it. He felt as if he were eating his last meal. The aura of danger and self-destruction which surrounded this strange young man could bring death and decay to anyone it touched. If he could only get away, he could fetch his family and be gone before nightfall.

"When do we leave on our journey?" he asked. "I must bid farewell to my wife and daughter. She always keeps a store of traveler's bread, for a merchant must often travel with little preparation. We live not far from here, and if you wish to leave before nightfall, I could easily return so that we could depart the city without fear of being observed."

"Those who leave immediately after eating are sure to suffer ill fortune on their journey," said the young lord, "but you may run, Manik, like a deer, and return to my fold before dark. And may not ill fortune attend your journey." He smiled at his own play on words, for the day name, Manik, also signified a deer. Every man had a nagual or animal double in the spirit world, which might serve as a protector or nemesis. Some men knew, or felt that they knew, the species of their animal partner, and accordingly would not eat the flesh of that animal, seeing such a meal as the equivalent of cannibalism. To pretend that Manik's double was a deer, just because he name also meant deer, was a silly conceit, the sort of teasing old friends might engage in. 8 Manik was far too preoccupied to take offense.

"I will return far before nightfall, my lord," he said, and backed toward the door. It was surprising that the noble would let him go so easily, for anyone would know that once out of sight 8 Manik would be free to flee this insane man.

"I will see you," answered the lord, "I am never wrong about these things."

Manik was careful to show no sign of hurry as he stepped from the doorway. He turned north, away from the direction of his home, and walked with what he hoped was the purposeful stride of a confident man who has much to do. Eyes rich with curiosity marked his passage -- the neighbors could not fail to be ignorant of the wealth of the strange household among them -- but no one seemed to follow him or tarry along the way when he slowed his progress. Gradually moving in a great arc, he worked his way west, and then south, moving toward the quarter where the vendors lived and he could find himself among those familiar to him.

His wife was waiting in the doorway of his compound, her face a mask of fear. She rushed at him the minute she saw him, moving with a strange limping gate, grabbing his arm so hard that he had to hold her up to keep her from falling onto the path.

"Where have you been?" she scolded, "Hunapu, our grandson, has been taken from us!"

"Is he dead?" shouted 8 Manik, aghast. "Has some accident befallen him? Why did you not watch him more carefully?"

"No." she screamed, incensed at his criticism, "He was inside the house. Three strange men burst in and seized him. I tried to stop them, but they pushed me away and sprained my ankle. I couldn't follow them. Our jewel, our heart, is gone!"

CHAPTER TWO

Motes of dust glittered in the afternoon sunlight as 8 Manik called his family together. All day the courtyard of his little compound had been full of frenzied activity – arguments, weeping, orders, and despair following one another in a welter of confusion, but now the family members fell silent as he took his place, sitting cross-legged on the packed, swept earth. The circle that formed included most of what 8 Manik loved in the world. His wife, Ch'en; his second son, Ix; his first son's wife, Kayab; and his daughter, Lamat. One place was empty. Muan, his oldest son, father of little Hunapu, was away on a trading expedition to Copan, far to the south. Smoke from the fires of neighboring compounds drifted through the chinks in the cornstalk walls bringing with it the smells of dinners being prepared, but there was no fire in 8 Manik's compound and no food either. The entire afternoon had been spent in the hunt for the missing child. 8 Manik could see despair and fatigue in the faces around him.

"I knew we shouldn't have let Muan name him Hunapu," moaned Ch'en. "It was a temptation to ill fortune. The night he was born I dreamed of a frog, but instead Muan insisted on giving him the name of a hero. What is a merchant's son doing with such a name?"

Kayab, her cheeks streaked by tears, leapt up to remonstrate her mother-in-law, but 8 Manik reached out and touched her on her arm to quiet her. This was no time to renew old battles within the family.

Ch'en's name was the word for "a well" and people with that name were supposed to be deep and quiet in nature, but the name ill-suited 8 Manik's wife. She was always active, working from morning until night, bustling from one side of the compound to the other. 8 Manik liked to tease that her true name was "waterfall" because she never stopped chattering. After years of marriage, he'd come to realize that she used her constant worrying as a way of warding off evil, as if predicting impending ill fortune gave her control over it. Only one of her children had died at childbirth, and her constant care had kept the others safe when 8 Manik was away on trading expeditions that might last three lunar cycles. "A trader's wife is a widow," the old saying went, meaning that she must learn to fend for herself, for a good merchant was always on the move.

"No one can undo the past," he remarked in gentle remonstrance. "Perhaps in the next cycle of the universe we will know how to name our children better."

"All of our neighbors say they have no idea which way the intruders left with Hunapu," burst out Ix, 8 Manik's second son. "It simply cannot be that no one saw. They're afraid if they tell us, the nobles will take revenge on them. I would have expected better from people in our own guild!"

"If only Muan were here," Ch'en burst out. "They would tell him, knowing that a father has a sacred bond with his child. He left for Copan six days ago. It will be another twenty before he returns."

"We know who took him," 8 Manik cut in. "The abduction can only be a way for forcing me to travel with the insane nobleman."

"Then why don't we go back to that house and free him?" burst out Ix. "I can't believe we haven't gone there already. I know a dozen men in the guild who would help us. We could storm the compound and save Hunapu."

"They might kill him!" said Ch'en. "Those men who came and took him would stop at nothing. I looked in their eyes. They were like blanks, with no souls inside. They stared right through me."

"But we must save Hunapu!" shouted Ix. "The members of a family are like the posts of a house. If one falls, the entire structure comes down. What good is a family if the members do not stand as one?"

8 Manik stood up. He had to quiet Ix's shouting. Ix was a good son and loyal to his older brother as a second son should be, but his impetuousness was always getting him into trouble. As 8 Manik stood, the group fell silent. He could feel them looking to him as leader. He must say the right thing or lose control entirely.

"Ix is right," 8 Manik began. "A family is a house. We all know this. But the posts of the house are beneath one roof, and the members of the family are underneath the father. The roof stands above the posts not to dominate them, but to protect them. If the roof does not tie the posts together, each falls in its own way. If we are to save Hunapu, and I believe we can, then everyone in the family must work together. To do that, they must be guided from above."

They all nodded their assent, but 8 Manik thought that Ix looked a little sour as he yielded to parental authority.

"First," 8 Manik continued, "The house cannot exist without the support of all its parts. Ix, you must travel south to find Muan and bring him here. The merchants that you meet who are returning north from Coban will give you plenty of information about his passage. Every vendor is sensitive to the comings and goings of his competitors. Tell them that our store of quetzal plumes was robbed, and I am pursuing the thieves to the north. Tell them that you, Muan, and I must unite so that we can find a way to restore our losses."

"Can't we send a messenger?" asked Ix impatiently.

"Muan might think that the messenger was trying to mislead him," said 8 Manik. "We are trying to maintain secrecy, but news this exciting would be all over Tikal. What is most important is to give a plausible reason why we are canceling our trip to Kaminaljuyu in the highlands immediately before they celebrate the 20'th anniversary of the ascension of their kalumte. Everyone in the guild knows that only a fool would miss such a market. All the noble families will be intent on have new feathered cloaks to display in the grand procession."

Ix settled himself a little more deeply on his crossed legs. 8 Manik hoped that his explanation would satisfy him. Ix had to be kept away from Tikal. If his fierce pride didn't get him into trouble, his impulsive tongue would.

"You women must cease your weeping and let the neighbors know the same story. We have to have some explanation for all the activity today, one that will get people talking but which doesn't excite suspicion. Tell them that we found Hunapu, that he had wandered off during the commotion surrounding the robbery, and that we thought he had been taken by the thieves.

"Won't the neighbors wonder where he is?" asked Ch'en.

"We will send Kayab to visit her mother in Uaxactun. We'll say that she has taken the boy with her."

"My baby," moaned Kayab. "I can't go so far from my son."

"Hunapu is alive," 8 Manik retorted. "He must be or the noble would have no way of ensuring my cooperation. He cannot take the boy north with us, for he must move quickly if he is to get to Palenque and back before a successor to Twin Jaguars appears in the great temple to receive the adulation of the people. He must send back someone to communicate to his allies that I am cooperating. Otherwise whoever is holding Hunapu here would have no way of knowing what action to take. When Ix returns with Muan, the two of them can watch the compound to see who comes and goes. By following them, they will uncover Hunapu's hiding place. Then they can arrange a raid with men of the guild to free him. A sudden strike at a moment when their guard is down is our best chance."

"And what will happen to you?" Che'en asked. "when the lord discovers that Hunapu has been recovered?"

"That is not a worry," said 8 Manik, with more assurance than he felt. "The noble has kidnapped Hunapu to ensure my cooperation. That means that he must need something that I can do which he cannot obtain in any other way. As long as I cooperate, he will have no motive to kill me. In any case, it is my will that I should go. The rain which falls must land on the roof of a house, not on the inhabitants within."

"But his plan is insane!" objected Ix. "A great lord is never alone. His stewards and his bodyguards are always with him. His strength is the strength of the city. There is no way that he can be killed by some crazy man from another place. This lunatic is leading himself, and you, to certain death. It is he that will be carried to the ball court to play a last, suicidal game with whomever the great lord chooses as his champion. It will be his body, bound and with its heart torn out, that will be thrown from the parapet of the ball court when the game is done. If you are caught with him, you will be sacrificed as well."

"I said I would leave with him for Palenque," said 8 Manik. "I never promised to arrive. You will catch up with Muan within five days, for you will be following him unburdened and he has no need of hurry. The two of you will be back within ten days, long before a party could begin to approach Palenque. I will take the opportunity to slip away then. You will have saved Hunapu before the news of my escape reaches Tikal."

"And if he catches and kills you after you escape?" Ch'en's appeared calm, but 8 Manik heard a tone in his wife's voice -- a hopeless, desperate quality that, for all her worrying, he had never heard before.

"I know the trading routes to the north far better than any noble ever could. There are a hundred short cuts along that path. His time is scarce, not mine. He must pursue his mad adventure and return. If he spends more than a few hours chasing me, he loses all. And if he sends back word to harm the boy, he will find me here before any messenger that he has could arrive.

Ch'en looked at him suspiciously, but she kept her peace. She would not argue with him in front of the rest, but he knew he would hear more from her in private. "I'll pack food for your trip," she said. The moment she stood up, the rest of the family circle felt free to move as well. With a sense of surprise, 8 Manik realized that without her tacit assent, none of the rest of the children would have obeyed him.

Ix moved to sit beside Kayab, reassuring her that the plan would work and the Hunapu would be back soon. "Think how fat he'll be, eating meat every day in the house of a noble," he said in a clumsy attempt at joking to cheer her up. "When he comes home, beans and squash will be too common for him. You'll have to force tortillas into his mouth."

The thought of her son eating threw Kayab into another fit of weeping. Ix looked in despair to 8 Manik, who could only gesture his helplessness in return. He walked to the cookhouse to bid farewell to Ch'en. Lamat, his daughter who had sat silently throughout the discussion, rose and caught his arm.

8 Manik's compound, while large by the standards of the trading guild, consisted of two separate rooms, which opened on the beaten mud courtyard, as if they were separate houses. An even smaller hut, across the patio, housed Muan and his wife and children. The larger room was used for sleeping at night and for receiving guests during family festivals. During the rainy season, the family congregated there for shelter from the downpours that came every afternoon. From the beams of the roof hung the stores of feather plumes that were 8 Manik's stock and trade. The kitchen

hut was smaller, and Lamat, Ch'en, and 8 Manik almost filled it when they squeezed in together.

"Father," whispered Lamat, "you must not go. This man is crazy. His spirit guardian has allowed his animal soul to wander far. He is being neglected by the gods for his impiety. Such a man would not hesitate to kill little Hunapu. He will tell you that the child is safe, but you will be throwing away your life if you go with him." Lamat spoke in a low and earnest voice, fearful of setting Kayab into new tantrums of weeping if her words carried out to the patio.

8 Manik winced at Lamat's words. In a city like Tikal, two rival systems of religion had developed. Her words could bring great trouble if they were repeated to the priests who performed the great public rituals. They insisted that the gods had ordained the great pageant of life at the beginning of time and that the universe was engaged in a long, repeated chain of events, reiterated again and again through cycles of growth and destruction. These cycles were evident in the recurrent patterns of the planets in the heavens, the passing of the seasons, and allowed men to determine the best times for making war, concluding peace treaties, and avoiding the disasters which constantly threatened the order of life. All a wise man could do was to anticipate the forces of nature and adapt to them as best he could.

Many peasants and craftsmen espoused a contrasting view. They believed that a spirit universe existed below the great mountains but above the underworld, Xilbalba, the domain of the dead. Here spirit keepers tended flocks of animals, each of which was the soul double of a living human above. If a man or woman lived an upright life, the keepers guarded the kindred animal, feeding them and insuring their safety and the health of the linked human being. The animal doubles of those who lived badly, in contrast, were allowed to wander free. Such animals exposed themselves to danger and their linked humans to madness, disease, and death.

8 Manik had little interest in the ideas of either the priests or the shamans who sought to appease the keepers of animal doubles with gifts of food and incense. He had worked too hard and come too far to believe that he was following some preordained path. He had little faith in the covert rituals of the shamans who sought to cure the sick and bring good fortune. He was, in short, neither a heretic nor a believer, being instead a man who lived each day as it came without worrying about the world around him.

"Lamat is right," Ch'en chimed in. "Those ruffians who stole Hunapu looked like wanderers. Their souls were missing. When I looked into their eyes, I saw nothing but blanks. There was nothing inside."

"Listen you two," hissed 8 Manik, trying to express his urgency while keeping his voice low. "It's true that we don't know what they have done to Hunapu. But Kayab cannot bear the shock of learning of her child's death right now. It could knock her soul right out of her body. We must get her close to her mother, because if a soul wanders, it often tries to return to where it was born and it may find her there. As for Hunapu, I don't know if he is alive or dead, but I will not give up without a fight. I can't defeat this man today, so I will try to trip him tomorrow."

"And if you fail, you will leave me here alone," said Ch'en, but her voice had lost its tremors of fear and a calm and threatening note had entered instead.

"Not alone," said 8 Manik. "I leave you with two fine sons and a daughter, a son-in-law to grow the food to feed you, and grandchildren to care for. You will nag them morning and night to make sure they do not lose their way. You are their spirit guide to care for them while I range away. I have left you alone in every year of our marriage and I never worried about our family once. I knew that you were caring for them."

"And I worried about you every day!" retorted Ch'en. "That is the lot of a trader's wife. Sometimes you were gone so long that the new moons equaled the fingers on my hand. All I had was gossip from some stray member of the guild. 'He's carrying jade to Monte Alban,' they would say. 'Your husband is a clever one.' There were times when I wished you were only fit for tilling the soil like a stupid peasant."

8 Manik looked to see whether Lamat would take offense at this, but she seemed not to have noticed. Her husband was a hardworking, gentle man, but no one in the family had any illusions about his intelligence.

"There is not much time left before sunset," said 8 Manik, "and we must act quickly. After Ix has left to find his brother and it is dark. I want you to begin moving our stock of goods out of the house. The moon is in its final quarter, so the first hours of the evening will be dark. Send to Cib, my trading partner, and have him come with an assistant to carry the feathers away to his compound in Uaxactun. If times get bad here, you will be able to flee to his house and have the wherewithal to survive. Cib is an honest man and I have paid his debts in the past when he had losses on his trips, and he has helped me as well. Once Ix and Muan have rescued Hunapu, the whole family must leave for his house, and I will meet you there."

Ch'en looked at him without speaking, then turned toward the raised cooking platform at the end of the kitchen. "I have traveler's bread which I made up six days ago before Muan left. Then it turned out that Kayab had made abundance as well. This supply will last you fifteen days at least." As she spoke, she lifted a string of blackened lumps of maize dough, a food which traders could carry for weeks without spoiling and which they could cook quickly by boiling water over a fire. Simple fare, but nutritious. It was on such fuel that the great trading networks, which stretched from ocean to ocean, were sustained.

Ch'en next produced a finely woven net bag, lined the bottom with a small square mat, and placed the traveler's bread inside. A woven blanket was tucked in on one side. Next she retrieved a new pair of sandals from behind a large pot used for cooking tamales. 8 Manik looked at them in surprise.

"I bought them for you as a present for the day your birth year became complete," she explained, "You might as well take them now. I won't have some noble sneering at the old ones you insist on patching year after year."

"New sandals will wear my feet raw," protested 8 Manik.

"Take them if you won't wear them. Neither of your sons has feet as small as yours, so no one else can use them. They may prove useful."

8 Manik grabbed her as she bustled past and put his arms around her. "I will come back," he promised, "and I will come back wearing my new sandals."

She pushed him away, but her touch was gentle. "If you do not stop talking like that, you'll have another woman lying on the patio, washing away our house platform with useless tears. Go out the back. If the others see you going, they will raise so many objections the sun will have set two hours before you break free."

8 Manik gave her a gentle squeeze, rubbed his hand on his daughter's head as a final blessing, and slipped from the house. Glancing over his shoulder, he saw that he had little time to tarry on his way to Twin Rabbit's compound. Those who had come to the city to witness Twin Jaguar's funeral were dispersing and 8 Manik found himself swimming against a current of peasants and artisans moving toward the poorer quarters at the edge of the city. None stopped to wonder why a man carrying a trader's pack would be starting on the road at such a late hour or questioned why someone would start on a trading journey carrying such a light load.

Pausing at the outskirts of Twin Rabbit's neighborhood, 8 Manik put down his pack, letting the tumpline over his forehead fall onto his shoulders, the way he had thousands of times through his years as a trader. To a passer-by he might seem to be resting, but he wanted to hide the flint blade he had palmed before leaving the compound. Gently he slipped it down under the woven mat at the very bottom. Merchants usually traveled in small groups, armed with obsidian pointed staffs, which proved useful in warding off thieves. 8 Manik had left his staff at home, for he was sure that the noble would never permit him to travel while armed. The flint blade was narrow and easily hidden. Somewhere on their travel, 8 Manik hoped to shape a piece of wood to serve as a handle and provide him with a serviceable knife.

As he settled the tumpline back in place, 8 Manik felt his spirits rise. Now that he was away from the family and no longer had to assure them that everything would turn out all right, he found he could think clearly. When Twin Rabbit was fool enough to drop his guard, 8 Manik might be able to slit his throat in the night, race back to Tikal, and take the household by surprise, saving Hunapu.

Such plans were desperate chances, ruled over by the fates that controlled the world, but 8 Manik had seen stranger things in his lifetime. He prided himself on his ability to land on his feet. His challenge was to go on, to persevere no matter what the difficulties, and to use his cleverness to overcome the advantages of others, never taking unnecessary risks but being willing, when the time came, to risk all. Bold traders always outlive their stock of goods, the saying went among vendors, but 8 Manik knew that it required a combination of prudence with a willingness to take risks to succeed.

He reached the noble's compound ten minutes before sunset and stopped to survey the entrance. Something looked out of place, but he couldn't quite identify what it was. The doorway was no different than any other. The thatched room was extraordinarily thick for the house of a potter, but the nagging voice in his brain said that that wasn't what was strange. He had seen the buildings earlier than the day and they looked as peaceful as the next, with the welcoming smoke curling up from the cooking fire within.

The smoke! Even as he watched, 8 Manik saw it build in intensity, coming not from the rear of the compound where Twin Rabbit's consort had done her cooking, but from the ceiling of the room directly in front of him. Within a few seconds, he saw flames licking at the gable and heard the crackle as the dry thatch flared. He ran headlong through the doorway of the compound.

Like all Mayan cities, Tikal lived in terror of fire. A city of thatched roofs set even in the steaming jungle was susceptible to the slightest spark. The palm fronds wet by the rain, then burned by the tropical sun, became brittle and flammable within a year or two. When they burned, the billowing up drafts carried sparks from one compound to another. At this moment, the still air of dusk allowed the smoke and sparks to rise directly upward, but an evening breeze could immolate half the city.

Bursting through the doorway, 8 Manik found Twin Rabbit holding a torch to the eaves of the kitchen house, even as the flames crackled up to the ridgepole of the larger reception room in which he and 8 Manik had dined. In the center of the courtyard, the beautiful young woman stood holding her child in her arms. At her feet, his scared eyes staring at the mounting flames, lay little Hunapu, his arms and legs bound behind him, screaming lustily.

Twin Rabbit glanced over his shoulder. "Your arrival is well timed, merchant," he said as calmly as if he were discussing the weather. "I was about to push that brat into the larger room before I left. You have saved his life."

8 Manik rushed to his grandson and snatched him up. The boy was struggling to free himself from the cords binding him. When he saw his grandfather, his screams lost a little of their intensity.

"You're insane!" 8 Manik shouted at the noble. "You could set fire to the whole city."

"Oh, I'm sure that my neighbors are already rushing to the reservoirs to draw water to dampen their roofs," said Twin Rabbit. "They will think first of preserving what is theirs long before they come to put out this fire. That is what is wrong with Tikal. The people are a rabble thinking only of themselves."

The cords around Hunapu's ankles came free and 8 Manik stood him up. Screaming even louder, the boy fell back to the ground. The cords had been bound so tightly that he had lost all sensation in his feet. For a second, 8 Manik had the impulse to sweep the boy into his arms and break for the doorway, but a glance showed that three burly young men barred the way. They must be the ones that had snatched Hunapu at the compound.

Cries of alarm from the neighboring compounds confirmed what the young man said. 8 Manik could hear mothers screaming for their children, men shouting wildly for water. The little group centering on Twin Rabbit was an island of calm, like the pause in the center of one of the great storms that swept across the land once in a generation bringing flooding and disaster.

"You're insane!" 8 Manik repeated. "Would you be the great lord of a city in ashes?"

"There is no wind to fan these flames," said Twin Rabbit contentedly. "A compound here or there doesn't interest me. Now is the time for us to depart. My concubine will take the boys to a place where they will be safe in case members of your family try to make a surprise raid and free them. Don't worry. Your grandson will be well cared for. She has a gentle heart and is most submissive to my commands, as you have seen. You and I and my three good servants will slip off to the north through the grove at the back of this building. She will leave through the entryway, part of the mass of women and children rushing to safety. No chance that any confederate of yours will be able to follow her in all this turmoil."

8 Manik dropped to his knees and smoothed Hunapu's hair as he looked into his eyes to soothe him. "You must go with this woman," he whispered to the boy.

Hunapu, his arms still bound behind him struggled to cling to 8 Manik, but the effort made him lose his balance and fall toward the dirt of the patio. 8 Manik grabbed him and hugged him. "Go with this woman," he repeated. "Your mother will come and find you later."

The young woman stooped down and swept Hunapu up in her arms, so that her own son and the merchant's grandson straddled her hips on each side. "I will keep him safe," she said, staring into 8 Manik's eyes. In her voice, 8 Manik heard the accents of the highlands far to the north. Without saying another word, she turned and walked through the billowing smoke and out the entryway, waddling with the weight of the two children. A gust of wind carried the smoke into 8 Manik's eyes, and when his vision returned she was gone.

"You should have found a wife like that," said Twin Rabbit. "The women of the highlands will do anything they are told. Maybe I will give her to you after I ascend the great pyramid."

"Would you have it said that your wife is more loyal and trustworthy than you are?" snapped 8 Manik, furious at the condescension of this lunatic. "I already have a wife who is a loyal and decent human being."

"She would be an impediment when I am lord," said Twin Rabbit. "Would Tikal accept a woman who spoke with such a barbarous accent? I will have no trouble finding another to take her place."

"And your son?" asked 8 Manik.

"He'll do until I sire one of more noble lineage. Now we must go." He turned and entered the thicket of trees at the back of the compound. 8 Manik, surrounded by the three thugs, had little choice but to follow.

CHAPTER THREE

Dawn was beginning to streak the sky before Twin Rabbit motioned to the group to halt. For hour after hour, as the dusk deepened into night, he had forced the pace, driving his men on with commands and threats. They traveled the main path that headed west from Tikal, a way so broad that two or three could walk abreast. At first they were carried along with a crowd of peasants who had traveled into Tikal to witness the funeral, but once night fell, the path was empty and those few people they did meet hurried by with nothing but a few muttered words of greeting. Night was a time of danger, and the stranger you met on the path was assumed to be a thief or brigand.

8 Manik had hoped that he would encounter another merchant along the way. When traveling vendors met, it was both good policy and good manners to stop for a conversation, no matter how urgent the errand. A merchant coming down the path could warn of hazards, describe the state of the markets in other cities, and tell of the comings and goings of mutual acquaintances. 8 Manik thought he might be able to send some sort of message back to the family. The hope had been unanswered, for most vendors, drawn to the city to profit from the crowds attending the ceremony, would stay through the night and leave on the next day.

In the darkness, 8 Manik let his mind keep rhythm with the steady shuffle of the group's footfalls. The route was as familiar to him as the courtyard of his house. He'd first come this way with his father at the age of eleven, trotting along until he was exhausted to keep up with the distance-devouring pace of a seasoned merchant. As the years followed one another, the routine of travel had made his journey easy, even when his pack was heavily laden.

Physically, the night's travel was no challenge to 8 Manik. Feather merchants traveled with enormous bales of plumage, as heavy as a potter's stock and far more cumbersome. This trip his feet felt light and springy, particularly when the path led uphill where he would normally have to dig his sandals into the dirt to gain purchase. By the time the moon rose, the brawny men who were his guards were stumbling with fatigue.

"I could lose them in the forest," thought 8 Manik. "In the daytime, these men could see to follow me, but in the dark I could find my way to another path and leave them far behind." The idea, while tempting, did not stay in his brain for long. Twin Rabbit would quickly arrange to have Hunapu killed. What worried 8 Manik more was what Ix would do when he returned to find Twin Rabbit's compound in ashes and the baby nowhere to be seen. Perhaps he had already raced off on the road to Copan to find his brother. Muan was the most even-tempered of the family, more so than 8 Manik, and might find some way to keep Ix from losing control of himself.

Tomorrow we will surely meet traders on the road, thought 8 Manik. I might be able to send my family a message. But what message could he send? He could continue to urge caution and patience, but that would do little good. He would have to trust his sons to make the right choice. This was a strange sensation for 8 Manik, who was accustomed to giving his sons commands and watching that they were obeyed. Most days he neither thought about, nor prized, his sons' obedience. It was simply what he, like any Mayan parent, expected.

"We will turn off the path here," Twin Rabbit announced, breaking 8 Manik's train of thought. "Cover your eyes, all of you."

8 Manik looked at his three companions and was surprised to see the solemnity with which they dug in their packs and produced long woven strips of cloth, which they wound around their heads. This must be something they had done before, he thought, and something, which had been impressed on them as vital to their well-being. Twin Rabbit pulled a blindfold from his own pack and walked back toward 8 Manik.

"Turn around," he ordered, and when 8 Manik was slow to obey, he roughly pushed his shoulder to twist him. The next minute the folds of cloth were bound over his eyes and he found himself standing, swaying slightly to keep balance, in total darkness. There was a pause for a period of nearly a minute,, then someone gave a piercing whistle, and the silence resumed.

At last, 8 Manik heard a soft rustle of branches and felt the breath of someone standing just behind him. Fingers tested the knot at the back of his head, untied it, and pulled it tighter. Short periods of shuffling followed, perhaps as the blindfolds on the other men were examined. The hands returned to lift his left arm and place his palm on the shoulder of someone in front of him.

"Walk slowly now," commanded Twin Rabbit, and the group groped its way forward.

Their route led though thick underbrush, for 8 Manik could feel twigs slashing at his calves and thighs. Beneath his sandals, he could make out the rough, half-rotted texture of broken branches fallen to earth. The man in line behind him stumbled, pushing 8 Manik against the one in front. The path rose, then dropped swiftly and the footing became even more difficult. Suddenly, the man in front of him tripped and his shoulder jerked from 8 Manik's grasp. As 8 Manik swiped wildly to grab a bush for support, his arm slapped someone walking beside him. He received a buffet on the back of his head in return.

"Keep your hands to yourself, grandpa," a coarse voice snarled, and a second blow cuffed 8 Manik's ear. The accent was strange. Perhaps the man came from the northern reaches of the Mayan lands in Chiapas. He was certainly no man of Tikal.

"Walk slowly now," a more measured voice came from ahead. 8 Manik, pressing into the back of the man ahead who had regained his footing, felt a second body pressing into him from behind. The bodies were slick with the sweat of the long night's march and the smell of stale perspiration was all around him. Tightly packed together, the group inched along for another quarter hour, edging down a steep slope, until 8 Manik felt a draft of air on his shoulders, as cold and fresh as the breeze of a mountain pass.

"I'm going into the mouth of the underworld," he said to himself, but to his surprise he didn't feel great fear. The Maya believed that caves connected the lower levels of the universe to the surface of the earth. Follow them far enough and you would reach Xibalba, the domain of the dead. Priests and shamans went into the caves to keep the lords of Xibalba at bay, but a common man would never set foot inside a cave, for he lacked the magical skill to defend himself. Who would want to travel to a land where skeletons ruled and rotting corpses littered the wayside?

"That's far enough." This was another voice with a strange accent, and it spoke with the careless self-confidence of someone who is accustomed to being obeyed. "Twin Rabbit, this is a strange army you bring me from Tikal. Three young toughs and an aged man?"

"My army will grow with the season, like the grain planted in freshly burned fields," said Twin Rabbit, and 8 Manik could hear the resentment in his voice. "One grain of maize can yield a hundred in return."

"Be careful where you plant your seed," the voice came again. "Crows may come out of the sun and pluck the tender plantlings from the soil." The speaker indulged in a self-satisfied laugh. "You may remove your blindfolds, soldiers of the Great Rabbit, and look upon your new home."

Manik grabbed the blindfold and pulled it down so that it hung around his neck. He had squinted, expecting the sting of the tropic sun in his eyes, but the light was dim. Looking around, he found himself inside a large, stone-lined cavern. The walls were smooth and rippling, with fluted columns rising from floor to ceiling, which sparkled with moisture in the light of the torches around them. He could hear constant, faint dripping from deep within the earth.

The room was filled with men dressed in crude loincloths who stood barefoot on the slick surface of the floor. These men were even shorter than 8 Manik, heavily muscled, with their hair cropped short. Many bore scars on their faces and arms, and more than one had lost an eye or ear in some fight long past. There were at least forty of them, crowding around the visitors, staring at them with hostile indifference.

"Brigands," muttered 8 Manik to himself, and a wave of revulsion swept over him. Outlaws such as these had killed his uncle and one of his brothers. They were the scourge of the traders, desperate men who left their homes to prey on travelers. Traders knew that it was useless to offer any bribe to these men, for they were in the habit of killing everyone they dealt with to escape detection. The great leaders in the cities might organize search parties to root out such bandits, but they were ignorant of the ways of the jungle and the result was a futile march in a useless show of force. The brigands simply disbanded to hide in the houses of peasants who feared retribution if they informed. Other farmers were disgruntled by tribute payments to the elite for ever more construction on the temples and palaces of the cities.

"Let me look at them," the careless voice commanded, and the circle of bandits pulled back to open a lane toward a raised platform carved into one wall of the cave. The man who sat there cross-legged wore the simple breechcloth of his followers, but he had a jaguar skin thrown over one shoulder. His face was broad and amiable, but there was a calculating glint in his eye that belied his casual manner. He was stocky and heavily muscled with bulging biceps and knotted forearms. 8 Manik knew he would not like to meet this man in a fight. His body looked solid, as if it would chip if you dropped him.

Twin Rabbit pushed past 8 Manik and walked through the line of silent, hostile brigands to the platform. He stepped up, so that for a moment he towered over the seated leader, then lowered himself to sit beside him.

"The only plucking which the crows will do in my presence," he said, his voice formal and stately in his choice of words, "will be to feast on the eyeballs of anyone who dares to oppose us. At the end of our venture, Naked Jaw, I will be the ruler of the greatest city on earth and you will be Lord of Uaxactun, its principal ally."

As the two men spoke, the members of the gang turned away and silently drifted into the shadows in the corners of the cavern, pretending to return to the routine of daily life. Some lay on the straw mats where they must have spent the night. Others pawed through a heap of garbage in the far corner, apparently looking for scraps from the night before. To the eyes of an outsider, it might appear that the conversation between Twin Rabbit and Naked Jaw was occurring in isolation, but 8 Manik noticed that the members of the band spoke little to one another. He had no doubt that they were as attentive as the three guards left standing before the platform. 8 Manik wondered what they must think of the liberties Twin Rabbit took with their leader. Surely his grand promises must seem as insane to the bandits as they did to him.

Naked Jaw eyed Twin Rabbit. "This project that you spoke of. Does it go well?"

"Nothing could be going better. You have heard, I am sure, of the funeral of my brother just yesterday. The period of mourning is barely underway. It will take two times twenty days to do the rituals that identify the successor. On the fortieth day, the new kalomte must ascend the trail of blood, writing with his bloody footsteps on the steps of the temple the promise of conquest which he will achieve through his days, renewing the soil of Tikal with the blood of a slain foe. When I become that man, carrying to Tikal the greatest treasure of all, the heart of its northern rival, our position will be secure."

"And this old one?" Naked Jaw pointed to 8 Manik by pursing his lips and lifting his chin, "he will take us to the great Pakal?"

"No!" Twin Rabbit's eyes flashed with anger, "I need no one to take us to the great Pakal, as you call him. I grew up in the sacred precinct of Palenque. No one knows its secret ways better than I. I was schooled at that old man's feet, trained to be the traitor of my natal city. Finding Pakal is no problem. Taking his heart will be the matter of an instant."

"So why do you need this man," asked Naked Jaw. "Did you bring him here to sacrifice to ensure good fortune in our endeavor?"

"The sacred precinct is no problem," said Twin Rabbit. "If that were all of Palenque, I would have no need of you, or you of me. You could simply march into the center of Palenque and take whatever you needed. We must find a way to the center of the city without exciting suspicion. What stranger is it that walks to the heart of any city and no one takes notice? A merchant, of course! Before the moon is full, Pakal will celebrate the anniversary of his accession to the throne. There will be a great ceremony. The crowds will be enormous and all the subaltern lords will be gathered in their finery to endorse the event. What better opportunity for a band of merchants to find their way to the center of the city? We will sleep in the inns that cluster near the temples. At night, when the guards are asleep or drunk with celebration, we strike, you and I."

"You have brought us a guide, then," said Naked Jaw. "How do you know he will not betray us? We cannot march in with our spears in hand or with our darts and atlatls at our sides. A merchant travels with nothing more than a staff. All he would have to do is cry out and we would be overwhelmed by the crowds."

"He will not disobey." Twin Jaguar lifted his eyes and gazed directly at 8 Manik. "I have something that he values as much as his life, and if anything happens, his grandson will die in an extremely painful fashion. He will teach us to disguise ourselves as merchants and lead us wherever we want to go."

Naked Jaw's glance followed that of Twin Rabbit, and 8 Manik was discomfited to find the two of them staring directly into his eyes. He was not used to being the object of such attention. The nobles who bought his feathers for their elaborate costumes preferred to have their retainers handle the bargaining for them, and would stand ostentatiously staring in another direction as the terms of the exchange were made.

"Well, merchant," said Naked Jaw. "It would appear that if I am to join this man, I will need not only my good fortune but also your cooperation to protect me. What do you say? Can I rely on you to smuggle us into Palenque without giving us away?"

"I can't say that you look very much like a merchant," answered 8 Manik, choosing his words with care. "A lizard may put on feathers, but that doesn't mean it can fly."

Naked Jaw threw back his head and bellowed with laughter. Twin Rabbit looked annoyed. "What are you saying, merchant?" he snapped.

"A merchant goes to Palenque with a heavy load of feathers and returns with a light load of obsidian blades. Feathers may be light and stones may be heavy, but a man must struggle under a burden going because the number of feathers needed to make his trip worth the effort is enormous. Pure volcanic glass from the mountains beyond Palenque of the same value could be wrapped in a woman's shawl, it is so costly. To obtain enough feathers for a band as large as this would require years of hunting."

8 Manik could see the color rising in Twin Rabbit's cheeks, but he continued on. "Forty feather merchants would never arrive at the same time to a market in Palenque, no matter how festive the occasion. If I were heading to Palenque and found that even fifteen other vendors were going that way, I would change my destination. There would simply be too much competition to receive a reasonable price for my wares. I would continue on to Tonina, and if that proved too crowded, I would send word to my wife and continue as far as Monte Alban if I had to."

"So you are saying that this is the plan of a fool?" Naked Jaw leaned forward; enjoying the trap he had laid for 8 Manik. If 8 Manik recanted, it would show that he was afraid, willing to say anything to stay alive. If he persisted in pointing out the idiocy of the plan, he wouldn't live to see the outside of the cavern.

"No," 8 Manik began. "It is the plan of a great noble, one who spends his days in the affairs of state. You or I could dress like merchants or peasants and possibly fool the inattentive, but such a great lord would betray, by the confidence of his stride, that he was born to no humble trade."

It wasn't clear from his glowering countenance whether Twin Rabbit was mollified by this flattery. Naked Jaw smiled broadly, however, clearly taking delight in the game of wits.

"But you do counsel us to abandon this plan," he pressed. "Might not its great, shall we say, nobility bring it to grief?"

"The plans of a true ahau, a great lord, are always great."

Naked Jaw pounced. "First you tell me that we will be easily discovered and overwhelmed. Next you tell me that it is a great plan. What exactly do you propose?"

"Those who travel to buy and sell are heavily laden," said 8 Manik. "But those who bring gifts travel light. If an embassy were to arrive at Palenque with gifts to honor Pakal the Great on the anniversary of his reign, it would have to be led by a great noble. The leaders of such expeditions travel with large numbers of servants and bodyguards, far more than are needed to carry the elegant gifts they bring. Such men travel well armed, not just to safeguard the wealth they present but also to demonstrate the power of the city making the donation. Such an expedition might be from someplace near the coast, like Naj Tunich for instance. These men could march to the center of Palenque without being challenged because their intentions would be assumed to be peaceful.

"And I would immediately be identified!" shouted Twin Rabbit, angrily. "Doesn't your plan ignore the fact that I was raised in the very sacred compound we are going to enter? There must be a hundred kinsmen and servants of Pakal who would recognize me in an instant."

"What I have said reveals my ignorance," replied 8 Manik, wondering whether the extreme servility he displayed might be mistaken for mockery. "But when I have witnessed such expeditions from afar, they often have arrived late in the evening so that the members will have an opportunity to groom themselves to make a proper show in the morning when they are presented in the courts of the great. If our party were to strike on the first night, they might press their opportunity before the identity of the great lord was discovered."

Naked Jaw slapped his knee with delight. "Not a bad scheme at all, old merchant," he exclaimed. "You make good sense to me. Perhaps you were a thief in an earlier life and fate has brought you back to rejoin your brothers."

"There is a certain logic to it, if the stars are right," Twin Rabbit admitted reluctantly. "I will ponder on this plan. Everything must be done to assure success." He paused, a little smile crept across his thin lips, and he continued. "No great lord would ever undertake a war without a sacrifice to propitiate the gods."

"If you think that drawing a cord with knotted spines through your tongue will help, go right ahead," said Naked Jaw, jovially. "I have learned to rely on myself and my men to make my way in the world, but perhaps that is because I was born to a peasant mother and not a great family. I am sure the gods would not waste their time on me. I'm happy if they ignore me as much as they can." He spoke as easily as if he were a prosperous farmer, sitting in the courtyard of an ample home, consuming alcoholic maize drink and rejoicing in the success of his family.

"That isn't what I had in mind," said Twin Rabbit. "My illustrious ancestor, Stormy Sky, never started a campaign without sacrificing one of his men to the gods. He never ended a campaign without personally dragging his rival chief to the base of a pyramid by his hair and removing a second heart to place upon the altar."

If 8 Manik thought the cavern was quiet before, it seemed a hundred times more silent now. No one shifted. No one seemed even to breathe. From the back of the room, the soft plink of a drip hitting a pool seemed to echo in the hall.

Naked Jaw and Twin Rabbit glared at one another. 8 Manik could see the two profiles as the men attempted to stare one another down. Naked Jaw's features were coarsened from the blows of many fights. Twin Rabbit's face was graceful, almost feminine, but the set of his jaw was no less determined.

"I know nothing of what Stormy Sky might have done," Naked Jaw said at last. "But it never made sense to me to do my enemy's work for him. It just makes my side in a fight one man weaker, and I don't have a single man to spare for the gods. If you wish to sacrifice, you must choose one of your own."

Twin Rabbit's head swiveled toward him and 8 Manik saw triumph in his eye. He had hoped that by replacing Twin Rabbit's scheme with his own, the two would have no more need for him as a guide. Now he realized that Naked Jaw had sealed his fate and that of little Hunapu as well, for he had no doubt that Twin Rabbit would send orders to have the boy eliminated.

Here was an opportunity for Twin Rabbit to demonstrate his status as a great ahau, as a "lord of life and death." A great ahau was not simply a powerful leader, he was a mediator between earth and heaven – the reincarnation of a former ruler who had survived a battle with the lords of Xibalba after his death and reemerged in human form. By sacrificing 8 Manik, Twin Rabbit would both reaffirm his status as superior to the rabble around him and punish someone who had made him look foolish. Naked Jaw, himself, might not be immune to being impressed by a human sacrifice.

"The sacrifice must be a worthy one," Twin Rabbit began, savoring the moment. "The blood of some imperfect being might anger the divine ones who control our destiny." He was looking directly at 8 Manik. "He might be a man wise enough to speak with the most exalted of the land. He must be without blemish or stain."

The noble reached into his cloak and produced the jade dagger he had shown 8 Manik the day before. "This instrument of death," he intoned, raising it high above his head so that all could see, "has been wielded by the lords of my house – Stormy Sky, Kan Boar, Makhina Chan, Jaguar Paw Skull, Double Bird, and Shield Skull. Their power flowing though me will serve to keep our lands inviolate." His voice rose as he enumerated the great lords of the dynasty.

"Look!" shouted Naked Jaw. "Look at the left arm of the merchant!"

"What?" Twin Rabbit's head snapped around toward the brigand chief.

"There's a scar on his left arm! I can see it from here!"

"What are you talking about?" Twin Rabbit's face was contorted with fury.

"You said 'a man without blemish.' The merchant is no such man. He is inadequate for sacrifice."

8 Manik held himself perfectly still.

"You'll have to execute one of your own or give up the sacrifice!" Naked Jaw pursued his advantage.

The three thugs shifted uncomfortably beside 8 Manik. What would Twin Rabbit do? Having announced a sacrifice, he would look foolish if he now backed down. If he struck down 8 Manik, he would have to retract what he said about requiring a perfect victim. But to sacrifice one of the three men in the room who were personally loyal to him would make him weaker still. 8 Manik could not believe he would do such a thing.

"I select Cimi, the youngest," Twin Rabbit announced. "His name means 'death,' and while he is smaller than the other two, his life is innocent."

"No!" screamed Cimi, bursting forward and throwing himself at the foot of the platform where the two leaders sat. "You can't do this. I am your cousin. You said that you would make me a cahal, under you."

"Strip him and make him ready," ordered Naked Jaw, hardly trying to conceal his disgust with this appeal.

The men in the room surged forward, like a pack of dogs suddenly released from their tethers. They swarmed over Cimi's prostrate, flailing body – dragging him off into the shadows at the back of the cavern. After the tension of the preceding moments, they seemed delighted to hasten him to his doom, a doom that they had all feared but moments earlier. They pushed and shoved like a crowd heading to witness one of the great sacred games in the ball courts of the city. There too the losers might forfeit their lives. In a great city, a sacrifice occurred at the top of a pyramid, far from view. Here it would occur close before their eyes.

"Sit with me while our friend attends to his duties," muttered Naked Jaw to 8 Manik.

Twin Rabbit rose with hauteur and marched to the center of the room. 8 Manik was motionless. He'd never before been asked to be seated on an elevated dais, even by one of the leaders of the merchant guilds when they met in private courts to discipline their fellow traders.

"Come up here," the bandit leader repeated. "Don't be afraid. We are all more or less equal here. You know what the old saying is, 'There are no titles among the creatures of the jungle.'"

Reluctantly 8 Manik stepped upon the dais, stooping to remove his sandals as he would when entering a house. He crossed his legs and sat, being careful to take the side across from the spot Twin Rabbit had occupied. Every muscle in his body began to quiver as the realization of the danger that he had faced crept into him.

"He's a man possessed, you know," said Naked Jaw, speaking softly to keep the conversation below the hubbub erupting from the crowd where the bandits struggled to prepare the hapless, flailing Cimi for destruction.

"Insane," whispered 8 Manik. "He kidnapped my grandson to force me to cooperate. What are you doing with such a lunatic?"

"The storehouses of Palenque are as rich as any in the world," said Naked Jaw. "If he can get us in, my men are strong enough and fast enough to get me out with more loot than we could obtain in a dozen years in the forest. How he gets himself out is his problem."

8 Manik looked at Naked Jaw, a welter of conflicting emotions washing over him until he almost felt dizzy. Brigands were cruel, rapacious, and selfish. They preyed upon peasant and merchant alike. At least a dozen of 8 Manik's compatriots in the guilds had been murdered by outlaw bands, probably some by Naked Jaw himself. His own father had disappeared just ten years before, as likely to have been killed by outlaws as by being hunted by a jaguar or bitten by a fer-de-lance. All his life he had hated and feared the outlaw bands, yet now he owed his life to Naked Jaw. It took no imagination to think that it would have been he, and not Cimi, who was the object of the attentions of the eager mob.

"You saved my life," muttered 8 Manik, grudgingly.

"The delegation bearing gifts was a good idea," said Naked Jaw. "I can always use men with good ideas. How did you get that scar, by the way?"

"Someone insulted my wife," said 8 Manik. "I'm a trader. If I get out of this alive, I will continue to be a trader."

A shout of triumph rang from the knot of men at the far side of the room. Cimi, screaming with terror was dragged to the open space before the dais. He had been stripped nude and daubed with a few streaks of blue paint, a clumsy imitation of the body paint covering the entire body of a true sacrificial victim. A shove on his shoulder sent his struggling body crashing to the floor. Two men on each arm and leg held him trembling and helpless on the ground.

A high, keening wail sliced through the clamor and Twin Rabbit advanced toward the struggling body. On his head he wore the enormous, plumed headdress of the Alligator God. Already one of the tallest men in the room, Twin Rabbit now seemed enormous. In his left hand he held a pale green statue, a ceremonial jade carved in the likeness of the god. In his right hand, the ceremonial jade knife glinted in the torchlight. The rest of the crowd drew back as he advanced, chanting words that none of them could understand.

"Here's our omen," muttered Naked Jaw to 8 Manik.

Twin Rabbit stopped before the body of the terrified young man, towering over the figure of the sacrificial victim and the crouching men who held him. Then he dropped down, like a falcon stooping to its prey. The arm holding the knife slashed downward and blood spurted as Twin Rabbit ripped him open from the breastbone to the belly. Again and again the arm rose and fell, as Twin Rabbit smashed at the rib cage. Cimi's screams were silenced as the chest was breached and replaced by the awful bubbling of blood through the gaping wound. Finally the knife clattered on the stone floor. Twin Rabbit plunged his arm into the cavity and tore at the heart, seeking to wrench it loose. With a grunt he pulled it free. Holding it aloft, he turned to the four cardinal directions, before placing it, in the pool of blood that spread around the body.

"A propitious sign that the heart is beating," Naked Jaw whispered to 8 Manik. "He botched the sacrifice though. I've seen priests in Yaxchilan do it with a single blow."

An incredible stench rose into the room, nauseating 8 Manik. In his terror, Cimi had defecated at the feet of his master.

The men in the room were staring at Twin Rabbit in awe. He stood, his chin thrust forward, luxuriating in their attention. You could almost hear the minds of the crowd thinking in hushed unison, "he truly is an kalomte, a lord and king."

"Clean this up," ordered Naked Jaw with disgust. "I hate it when men crap when they die. We have to sleep in this room tonight."

CHAPTER FOUR

Exhausted as he was, 8 Manik found it impossible to sleep in the long hours of the day that followed. At Naked Jaw's order, the body had been dragged away and the offal washed from the floor with great jars of water from some source within the cave. The cool draft that flowed through the room carried away the stench of the sacrifice. 8 Manik lay on the woven mat which a bandit had spread for him and watched the slow routine of the room from half-closed lids. A throbbing headache pulsed at his temples. His arms and legs were heavy from the exercise of the night before, but too much had gone on since he first met Twin Rabbit at the procession for his mind to stop racing.

The men he saw moving through the cave were shabbily dressed, but they carried themselves with the proud confidence of men with far more property or status than simple peasants. It was difficult to identify anyone other than Naked Jaw who exercised any authority among them. The air was full of easy joking and buffoonish pranks. Many, like Naked Jaw, had accents from the mountains of Chiapas to the north and west, but some spoke like men of Tikal and the surrounding lowland communities.

As the hours wore on, the room gradually emptied. Men came or left singly or in groups of two or three, though on what errands, 8 Manik had no idea. Twin Rabbit had withdrawn deep into the cave, presumably to sleep out of sight of the rabble, and his two remaining followers had accompanied him. 8 Manik could only wonder what they thought of Cimi's death, since they might have been the one chosen for sacrifice as well. The act had clearly impressed the bandits, however, and they gossiped about it in hushed tones.

"This man must truly be a great leader," said one sitting not far from where 8 Manik lay, pretending to sleep. "He ordered the death of his kinsman without a thought."

"They say those who die in the service of a lord are ensured a safe path through the underworld," replied his companion, a squat fellow whose voice suggested that he came from the lowlands and whose chin bore a jagged scar.

"That's only true if you accompany a lord into his funeral chamber," said the first. "I'd rather stick with Naked Jaw than this one. Naked Jaw has his fits, but a least the people who stick with him live to see the next day."

"If this new guy works out, we could all end up as lords in his kingdom," said scar chin, "That's better than spending your life in the forest with Naked Jaw."

"I'll believe that when I see it," replied the first. "You and I will never sit on a dais, but if there's plunder to be had, I'll follow Naked Jaw."

They moved out of earshot. 8 Manik was surprised at their open questioning of their leaders and the way that they acted as if obedience were a choice instead of an obligation to those above them. He wondered how any group so lacking in reverence for its leader could prove effective. Still, as all the traders knew only too well, the bandit gangs were successful in flaunting the will of the proud lords who dominated the cities. Old people said the bands had never been so large and rapacious, but then old people always said that times had been better in their youth.

8 Manik's body ached with fatigue. His arms and legs felt heavy. He knew that he should sleep to gather strength for the days ahead and he tried to will his body to rest. It was no use. He could no more make his body sleep than he could make himself young again.

Finally his mind began to drift from one thought to another. His wife's parting words, so full of resentment about the time he had spent away from home, had surprised him. He hadn't had the slightest clue that she felt that way. And what good would it have done her to tell him? He knew vendors who had tried adopting some craft. Usually they were men who feared the danger of the constant traveling of the merchant life. Sometimes it was men experiencing sickness or lameness that made long journeys impossible. He'd regarded them as fools. He loved the life of a merchant in which each day brought new prices and new opportunities. Once when an unexpected shaking of the earth brought panic, he'd bought a load of salt from an idiot who thought the world was coming to an end. He'd carried it back to the coast, where salt was, naturally, cheap, and was able to sell it for double what he'd paid and still give his customer a good price. His companions had told him he was crazy and called him Saltfeather all the way back, but it was the profit on that coup that enabled him to set his daughter and her husband up with enough land to be self-sufficient. Now the same men told the story in hushed tones of respect.

He was drifting into slumber now, and the memories of that journey took shape in his mind. He was back in Tikal and little Hunapu hadn't been born yet. Like cacao beans and maize, salt sometimes served as a medium of exchange and he'd just completed a trade for some really fine quetzal plumes. Ch'en was beside him, telling him what a fine bargain he had made. His children were there and an old woman who must be his mother, even though she had died at his birth, all praising him as a magnificent trader. He was embarrassed by all the adulation, but he kept looking for his father because he wanted to hear this man of so few words join in the chorus of admiration. He pushed through the market to the place where his father always stood, but the spot was empty.

Finally, 8 Manik saw the bent shoulders of his father, staggering under an enormous load, leaving the market. He rushed to him and tapped him on the shoulder, but when the figure turned, 8 Manik saw not the familiar face, but the mask of the god Ek Chuah, the North Star, the Black Scorpion, patron deity of traveling merchants. Stunned, 8 Manik fell to the ground before the mighty figure.

"Today you have purchased salt," thundered the god, or was it a priest standing behind the god's mask? And it wasn't true. 8 Manik hadn't purchased salt that day; he had traded it away. But what did one say to a god (or a priest, for that matter) who had made a mistake?

"I fertilize the ground with the salt of my blood," the voice thundered. "Yet where salt falls to the ground, nothing can grow. Death gives way to life. Life grows ever from death. The old life must pass away so that the new life may grow."

Even in his dream, none of this made sense to 8 Manik. Everyone knew that the kalomte must come forth to the fields to renew the fertility of the soil with their blood. Without that ritual, the ground would grow barren. These were the great ceremonies, the eternal demonstration to trader, peasant, scribe, and potter that they could not survive without the great lord.

"Everything will be as it once was," thundered the god.

Crouched in his dream below the towering figure, 8 Manik found himself before the feet of the god. They were clad, not in rich, ornate sandals, but were bare on the ground, with the dirty, broken nails of a peasant who toiled in the fields day after day. The feet were filthy. This was no noble carried about on a litter by those beneath him. Before his eyes, the feet began to change. They were growing claws and the skin became scaly, like the feet of a lizard. 8 Manik resolved to run, but found he was rooted to the earth.

"Save me," he shrieked, not knowing to whom he was calling or what kind of salvation he expected.

From nowhere, a figure leaped upon the masked man or god, smashing at its chest. It was Twin Rabbit and he was pounding the body of the lizard-god with the jade he'd used during the sacrifice in the cave. The lizard coiled around Twin Rabbit's leg, trying to throw him down, but he kept his balance and hacked away again. Finally, with a cry of triumph he reached to rip forth the heart, but when he withdrew his hand and raised it aloft, it held the bright shining evening star. For a moment, the noble stood before 8 Manik in triumph, but then the dream dissolved. 8 Manik found himself groggy and awake.

He had no idea how long he had slept. He thought that it couldn't be close to dusk, or he would see sunlight slanting through the doorway of the cavern. It comforted him to think this, but he had to admit that, unless the door faced west, the opening was so small and the forest cover so dense that the change in light wouldn't be noticeable. Still, even thinking that he might be able to orient himself during the day was better than having no idea where or when he was.

As he lay on his mat, he tried to understand the meaning of his dream. 8 Manik was not a man who dreamed often and when he did, the dream disappeared from his mind almost as soon as he awoke. He knew that dreams are no idle fancies. They are communications from the supernatural forces that pervade the world. This dream must be a message, perhaps from the gods themselves. On the rare occasions when he did remember a dream, he would report it to Ch'en. She never failed to provide an instantaneous explanation.

"Dreams go by opposites," she would say. "Water means that good fortune is following. When a bird sings in your dream, it means that someone close to you will die soon."

None of these formulas were of any help in this particular dream. 8 Manik felt as he did when he stood before one of the great stelae, the carved limestone slabs erected in Mayan cities to commemorate significant events. All around the perimeter of the image of the ahau or god were elaborate glyphs whose meaning seemed more important because it was so obscure. Scattered throughout were the bar and dot numerals which everyone understood, counting with perfect exactitude the passage of days in the great cycles of time from one creation to the next. This dream too must be a communication of intense meaning, but he was as puzzled as a child listening to its parents' conversations and not knowing what to make of their utterances.

Somewhere in the dream Ek Chuah had become Kulkulkan, the god of the morning and evening star. Some said he had stolen the secret of maize from the gods and given it to mankind. In the highlands, the people believed that the sun and the morning star were rivals, battling for dominance in the sky. Some Mayans felt that the hero twins who defeated the Lords of Xibalba had become the sun and the moon to rule over the day and night. Others contended that the twins had become the sun and the evening star. Could the masked figure be little Hunapu, in his incarnation as Kulkulkan? Was Twin Rabbit's kidnapping the attack? Did the dream mean that Hunapu was already dead?

Still, these ideas did not seem right. The heart of the morning star as it shone in Twin Rabbit's hand was vibrant and alive. It had survived his attack, even as Twin Rabbit had exulted in his victory. The heart had been killed and reborn. Cycles upon cycles. The world itself had been destroyed and reborn. Ek Chuah had said that everything should be as it once was. That couldn't be true if Hunapu were dead.

The more 8 Manik tried to interpret the dream, the more confused he became. If only Ch'en were here, she would come up with some sort of explanation. Only one thing was clear. The gods did not deal in trifles or waste their efforts on the actions of traders and peasants. In receiving this message, 8 Manik was assured that this trip was no minor incident. If the gods were interested, then the fate of nations must be at stake.

8 Manik looked at the opening again and saw that the light had dimmed as he was pondering the meaning of the dream. Evening must be coming on. If the band were departing for Palenque, they

would probably leave under cover of darkness, yet there was no bustle of preparation around him. They would probably stay another day, but they would have to leave soon or they would have trouble keeping to Twin Rabbit's schedule.

The spot of light cast by the doorway blinked out and reappeared again. In the deepening gloom of the cavern, 8 Manik could see the silhouette of Naked Jaw coming toward him. Exchanging a friendly word or two with the men he passed, he worked his way toward 8 Manik's pallet. 8 Manik closed his eyes and tried to relax all his muscles to convince Naked Jaw that he was asleep.

A foot prodded his ribs, though not in an unfriendly manner. "Get up, merchant," said Naked Jaw, his voice calm and self assured. "I wonder what kind of success you could have had as a trader if you slept so long. Get up and come with me."

8 Manik made a show of startled stretching before clambering to his feet. He followed the sturdy figure across the room and stooped, as Naked Jaw did, to push his way into the greenery that screened the mouth of the cave. Outside, he found himself near the foot of a small ravine with an indifferent trickle of water flowing past his feet as it wended its way to the foot of the slope and lost itself in the underbrush. The sky had turned a deep blue with snatches of rose colored sunset visible though the trees at the western horizon.

"This is an excellent place to hide your band of men," 8 Manik ventured to Naked Jaw. "Close to the paths of trade, yet invisible to the expeditions sent from the cities to hunt you down."

"Anyone who lived in the forests would have little enough trouble finding it," said Naked Jaw. "Not even an animal can push through foliage without leaving marks that are plain enough to a hunter. Think how much more damage a human does. It doesn't do much good to hide in a cave, either. All a pursuing group has to do is camp in front of the doorway until we run out of food, and then pick us off one by one as we emerge. Of course, no ahau would ever listen to a common peasant or deign to ask his way when he is lost. So they send their armies up and down the roads and we are secure enough."

8 Manik tried to interpret the expression on Naked Jaw's face. He was staring across toward the hilltop on the far side of the ravine as he spoke, and his eyes wandered purposefully along the ridgeline. His tone was careless and casual on the surface, but 8 Manik suspected that a bandit does not joke idly about security, just as a trader does not joke about the state of the marketplace. 8 Manik suspected as well that there must be another exit to the cave, perhaps not even known to the men of the band, and certainly kept from Twin Rabbit. Naked Jaw would never allow himself to be trapped as easily as his conversation indicated.

Something stirred on the crest of the hill behind them. Naked Jaw's head snapped around, but then he relaxed. "The sentry," he said, offering no further explanation.

As darkness fell, the birds resumed their hurried patterns of flight and sociable calling to one another in the canopy of the jungle far above. A roar, louder than that of a jaguar, echoed down the narrow valley – the call of the howler monkey asserting a territorial claim. 8 Manik took a deep breath, taking in the smells of the jungle. Beneath the fragrance of flowering plants, he could distinguish the acrid musk of a javelina in heat and the undercurrent of fungal rot and decay. The smells of the jungle were like the undisciplined interaction of the men -- dozens of lives working at cross-purposes but linked in a common activity. Still there was a heady hint of liberty unknown in the crowded neighborhoods of Tikal. Maybe it was that freedom that drew him to the merchant life, the option of choosing one's path to profit or fail on one's own.

Enchanting as the free life might seem, its disorder was disturbing to 8 Manik too. He was, he had to admit, a child of the city. As he dominated in his compound, so too each ward and neighborhood had its place in the orderly march of time. When he died, his sons would head their own compounds, under the eye of an ahau whose position, like theirs, was largely determined at birth. Over kalomte, ahau, trader, and peasant was the domain of the gods, and even they were not eternal, for when this world ended in cataclysm, they too must be replaced in a new order.

Naked Jaw was like no leader he had ever known. He treated his men with easy cordiality. His conversations were amiable and unthreatening. Still, the men responded quickly to his requests and never seemed to lose their attentiveness to him. 8 Manik had to remind himself that this man lived by killing. His actions, and those of men like him, constantly threatened the trade of the entire Mayan area. Clever as Naked Jaw might be, 8 Manik could only disapprove of him.

"We won't move until tomorrow night," said Naked Jaw, as matter of fact as a vendor in his stall. "If my hunters don't have better luck, it may take another day after that."

"And then we're off to Palenque?" asked 8 Manik, desperate for whatever information he could worm out of the bandit leader.

"The men are eager to go," said Naked Jaw. "The sacrifice truly impressed them."

"It was a shoddy job," said 8 Manik. "I can't remember when I've seen worse. The priests at Tikal would have one of their number impaled for botching the use of the ceremonial blade so badly."

"Country folk have a hard time getting close enough to a pyramid to see the great sacrifices. For them, the death is enough."

"What does Twin Rabbit think of his performance?" asked 8 Manik. "He above all should be familiar with how it is done."

"He told me what a wonderful job he had done," said Naked Jaw, a dry cynicism evident in his voice. "Of course, the fact that he had to tell me might suggest that he knows he performed poorly."

"Double Bird," said 8 Manik.

They both knew what he meant. Everyone in the Maya world from the Caribbean coast to the mountains of Guatemala and Chiapas knew the story of the unhappy ruler of Tikal. Handsome, born to rule it seemed, but when he appeared for his first sacrifice, his blow went wildly awry. The sacrificial blade caromed off the rib cage of the intended victim and slashed his own thigh. Less than a year later, Tikal fell to armies from Teotihuacan, and a man who did not even speak the language of the people, son of the king of Teotihuacan, sat upon the royal dais. The gods had withdrawn their favor from Double Bird, though whether they had done so because he struck poorly or whether his blow went awry because they had withdrawn their favor, no one could ever know.

"You have killed many men," said 8 Manik. "Would it have taken you so many blows to dispatch the captive?"

"It is difficult to compare," said Naked Jaw, dispassionately. "I've never killed a man who was my ally. When the priests sacrifice a victim, they splay him over a curved altar that forces his chest upward. That would make the blow easier. I never aim for the body. A slash across the throat is far more lethal. Any jaguar will tell you that."

Was Naked Jaw hinting that the jaguar was his spirit double? In the deepening twilight, 8 Manik stared at Naked Jaw's face, trying to read the emotions there. He spoke about killing as a potter might speak of making a complex and difficult piece, with the specialist's concern for technique. Did jaguars experience a similar sensation when hunting their prey? On the other hand, Naked Jaw might simply be cultivating the idea of a jaguar spirit double to impress his men.

"Let me go from here," 8 Manik said impulsively, but being careful to keep his voice low. He knew better than to plead with the bandit leader. Pleading just invited domination from a man of power. A simple argument was needed, one that appealed to Naked Jaw's self interest and the needs of his group.

"I have already saved you from that empty-headed scheme of posing as a band of merchants," he began. "You owe me thanks for that, if nothing else. You have no need of my knowledge now. Once Twin Rabbit leads you to the center of Palenque, I would be a hindrance, not a help. I have no skill in battle, if it comes to a fight. You even run the risk that I will betray you all if the opportunity arises. Just give me a day. Moving with speed, I can be back in Tikal by noon tomorrow. You could tell Twin Rabbit that you sent me on some errand under guard."

"And when he discovered you were gone for good?"

"I would have a day at least before the news reached Tikal. That might be time enough to find the boy. Any trader knows how rumors fly and how to read conflicting tales to assess the situation. I would have a chance. Once I found the boy, I would flee south. And I would not betray your plan. Who would believe me if I did? What does a simple trader know of lords and bandits?"

Naked Jaw threw back his head and guffawed. The sound was not unkind, but it suggested little hope for 8 Manik's entreaty. "I'm not worried about you betraying this plan. Who would you go to? Tikal has no kalomte. Twin Jaguar's funeral occurred only yesterday. If we start in the next two days, no party could be organized to catch us. And why should Tikal worry about the security of its a rival ruler? Lord Pakal is hated well enough in your fine city."

"All the more reason to let me go, if there is no risk," persisted 8 Manik.

"You can betray Twin Rabbit if you wish. It's not important to me. I live my life dodging from one chance to the next. I'll land on my feet whatever becomes of this mighty lord or that. I'm worried that you will betray me."

"How could I lead anyone here?" 8 Manik's pressed on. "You blindfolded me on my way to this place. Your men could blindfold me on the way from it."

"You wouldn't have to know where my cave exists," said Naked Jaw. "You only need to know that it exists. Don't swear me any oaths. We both know the business I'm in. Three years from now when members of your guild lie dead, friends or relatives, would you be able to stop your tongue? Once people know there is a cave, will they not find it when they seek for it? No, I cannot let you go."

"Then why not kill me now?" flashed 8 Manik in anger. "Nobles love to boast of their acts of generosity. Perhaps this wild man's wife would intercede for my grandchild and soften his heart. With me dead, the boy is of no further use, and he is no danger. That might be my best chance of all."

"You are of no use to Twin Rabbit," said Naked Jaw, seeming to enjoy the play at cross-purposes. "But you are of use to me."

8 Manik retreated to bitter silence. He knew Naked Jaw was waiting for him to ask why, and he refused to give him the pleasure of submitting to his teasing.

After a long pause, Naked Jaw went on. "Twin Rabbit knows the ways of Palenque. You have sold in the market there many times. I am a creature of the forest. When I was a child I was taken to Bonampak to witness the accession of a lord. I have been in Yaxchilan once, but I try to keep as far from cities as possible. A bandit must act from a position of overwhelming power. A band of forty armed men confronting an expedition on the road cannot be resisted. In a city, there are thousands – thousands to see your approach, thousands to inform the leaders, thousands to resist. If Twin Rabbit leads me to the sacred precinct in Palenque and then is killed, how am I to escape?

You have spent your life traveling in and out of cities. You would prove a useful guide."

I was right, thought 8 Manik. There must be a second entrance to the cave.

"And I do have something to keep you loyal," said Naked Jaw. "I know where your grandson is hidden. You might search Tikal all you wish and never find him. He has been taken away from the city. He could be in one of a hundred villages."

As they talked, the dusk faded. The evening star, Kulkulkan, shone in the deepening blue of the newborn night. Most brilliant of the wandering stars, harbinger of war and death, it twinkled brilliant in the western sky above the far side of the ravine. It was the most beautiful, most dangerous, companion of the sun and rival at the same time, never straying far in the heavens, alternately leading and following its mighty lord. Had he instructed Ek Chuah to carry the message in that dream for 8 Manik to decode?

"Where salt falls to earth, nothing can grow," he muttered to himself. Then he realized that everything Naked Jaw had said about knowing that the cave existed applied no less to Twin Rabbit than to himself. What lord of Tikal would allow bandits to prey upon his trading ventures if he could prevent it? The urge to surprise Naked Jaw and obliterate him would be an imperative that none could resist. Once Twin Rabbit led Naked Jaw into the sacred precinct of Palenque, the bandit had best watch his back. The blood of more in the cave would water the soil before his expedition was done.

CHAPTER FIVE

The hunters returned the next afternoon with only a half-grown tapir and two capybaras to show for their efforts. They came through the doorway of the cave, emanating failure in their every gesture and filling their conversation with disgust at the scarcity of game in the region. Twin Rabbit, who had returned to the dais to receive the bounty of the forest, was wild with contempt. Naked Jaw sat in silence as the young noble berated the hunters.

"Scarcity of game," he stormed. "I have hunted these woods before and never failed to return without at least two deer and sometimes as many as a dozen other animals. There's nothing subtle about hunting. You simply have to travel until you see an animal and then kill it. You men, more than anyone, should be counted on to have skill with the bow and spear thrower. You spent the first day of your hunt wasting time by some spring waiting for the animals to come to you."

"No, my lord, we," began one of the hunters, but Twin Rabbit cut him off.

"Don't think you can fool me with foolish excuses. I know a liar when I see one. You should admit to your failures honestly. If you spent the time hunting you did cooking up your stories, this cave would be full of meat."

The men stared at their feet and made no response.

"My plan was to leave tomorrow! We must arrive in Palenque by the appointed date. Everything depends on being there. You ignorant peasants don't understand these things, but the stars must align or our plan will never succeed."

"There's still time," Naked Jaw broke in. "My men will find game tomorrow. One day the hunting is good, the next day it isn't."

"See that they do!" snapped Twin Rabbit and stamped off to the deeper recesses of the cave.

8 Manik thought that Naked Jaw must be humiliated to be ordered about in front of his men, but all the leader said was, "Try going north tomorrow."

Late that evening, when most of the men of the band were asleep, Twin Rabbit reappeared and staggered toward the dais, carrying a pitch pine torch. "Sorry I acted like that," he muttered in the general direction of Naked Jaw, but his eyes focused on no one in particular. "Hunting better tomorrow. No need to fear." He tried to step up on the dais, but his foot slipped and he struggled to maintain balance. In the end, he slipped to a sitting position with one leg on the edge of the platform and the other stretched out before him.

Naked Jaw gave him a sharp glance. He had been quiet the whole day, apparently lost in thought. All he said was "Hunting is good one day; the next it is bad."

"No!" Twin Rabbit's voice grew louder, even petulant. "I shouldn't have spoken as I did. I know that now."

"Quietly," whispered Naked Jaw. Some of the sleeping men stirred. Those who were still awake were straining to eavesdrop. From his spot near the dais, 8 Manik could see that Twin Rabbit's eyes were bloodshot, with a blank stare that swept wildly about the room.

"Tomorrow the hunting will be better," repeated Twin Rabbit. "I know. He told me."

"Go to sleep," said Naked Jaw, as gently as a mother talking to a fretful child.

"Do you want to know how I can be sure the hunting will be better?" asked Twin Rabbit, petulantly. "I traveled to see him, the rabbit that lives in the moon, the one for whom I am named."

He can't have seen the rabbit in the moon, 8 Manik thought. You can only see the rabbit when the moon is full. We are just a few days before the new moon appears as a crescent. The moon won't rise until just before dawn.

"I traveled there," Twin Rabbit repeated. "I am always welcome on the moon. The rabbit on the moon loves me more than all who bear his name."

"You may travel where you will and when you will," said Naked Jaw. Although his voice had become no louder, no one could avoid the edge of command, even menace, in the way he clipped his words. "Just make certain that you keep the cave clean. It is an ill bred bird that fouls its own nest."

He's using the mushrooms, 8 Manik thought. Who does he think he is? Only the greatest ahaus can practice those spells.

"Everything fine tomorrow," slurred Twin Rabbit, staggering to his feet. "Hunting good tomorrow."

Naked Jaw's look of loathing, which followed Twin Rabbit as he retreated deeper into the cave, was matched by 8 Manik's own. Certain mushrooms were sacred, to be used only for communication with the gods. They were mixed in a potent alcoholic brew and administered as an enema. They gave the users supernatural insight, opening their minds to communications from the gods which enabled the leaders to predict victory in war or the coming of disasters such as hurricanes, earthquakes, or eclipses of the sun. Such knowledge was powerful and dangerous. Some said that the mushrooms would kill commoners who attempted to use them. Many believed that the forest dwellers that collected them and brought them to the courts also used them to enhance their sexual powers. Those who made repeated use were said to grow depressed and subject to seizures.

No problem of mine, thought 8 Manik, and curled himself more tightly on the straw sleeping mat.

The next morning brought more trouble. The carcasses that the hunters brought in the day before had disappeared. They had been placed near the opening of the cave so that the outflow of air would carry their stench away from the sleeping band and now they were gone without a trace. Consternation reigned in the cavern. Naked Jaw stalked up and down the room, glaring at his followers, attempting to detect a guilty look in the face or bloodstains under the nails to identify the culprit who had stolen them. One unfortunate young man suggested that a jaguar might have crept into the cave to drag away the fresh meat.

Naked Jaw exploded in fury. What jungle animal would ever enter a place where the smell of man was so strong? It would be a clever animal indeed that could walk on the floor without leaving footprints. Maybe the young man thought that a buzzard had flown in during the night and carried the meat away.

"Monkeys?" the youth suggested, only to provoke new waves of scorn.

Very quiet monkeys, Naked Jaw began. Monkeys that moved during the night instead of daytime. Meat eating monkeys, there was something new. No, some man had stolen the provisions from the cave and he intended to find out who and why.

Throughout the inquisition, Twin Rabbit sat on the dais, morose and withdrawn. 8 Manik crouched nearby, trying to look as insignificant as possible.

Naked Jaw's insistence that it had to be a man who stole the meat led him down paths that were ever more baffling. No one who stole the food could have eaten it. The Maya never ate meat raw, and someone who lit a fire in the night would have been spotted by the watchmen who were posted in the surrounding forest. None of the three men had seen any sign of fire or any unusual movement of animals startled by the thief. In the end, Naked Jaw had to be content with sending out extra parties of hunters, fanning them in all directions, hopeful that one of the bands would stumble on a herd of deer and gather sufficient numbers to support them on their journey.

While Naked Jaw stormed through the cavern, Twin Rabbit retained an uncharacteristic silence. "The hunting will be better today," he predicted.

The hunting wasn't better. The parties returned with nothing more to show for their effort other than a few birds that they had managed to snare. Naked Jaw looked at the meager production and his face was like a mask.

"We'll leave tomorrow, anyway," he said. "There are a hundred villages between here and Palenque. They will be happy to share their food with us as we pass along our route."

8 Manik knew that the happiness involved in this sharing would be decidedly one-sided. Most

peasants lived in small hamlets to be near the fields that they tilled, widely dispersed from their neighbors. A village might have a total population of thirty or forty people, including women and children. What defense would such a community have against a band of over forty men out to steal everything they could carry?

The men accepted the news stalwartly enough, shrugging and turning away to go about their business. It was all the same to them. Of course, 8 Manik realized that a major part of Twin Rabbit's scheme, arriving without prior warning, had gone awry, but it need not be disabling. If any of the men wondered why Twin Rabbit's confident prediction of success in the hunt had gone wrong, they didn't voice their skepticism.

The next morning the band was up before dawn. The bustle and informality of the preceding days was abandoned, as the men squatted in silence, wolfing down the remains of the evening meal. Some tended to their weapons, tightening the binding of a spear point or rewinding a bowstring. They didn't look worried, but 8 Manik felt that few were relishing a long march to the west.

Outside, the air felt as dank as the interior of the cave, but it was warm and fetid. Only an occasional shaft of sunlight pierced the mists that clung to the trunks of the forest trees. The bandits became even quieter, huddling together in the dim half-light, waiting for Naked Jaw to order the start of their journey.

Twin Rabbit emerged from the cave last and looked around with an air of anticipation notably lacking in the company around him. "So it begins," he announced to no one in particular. "The gods and our good strong arms will ensure success."

There was still no response from the surrounding men.

"Today will long be remembered by the scribes of Tikal," declared Twin Rabbit and waited expectantly for a shout of approval. "We restore the rulership to its true, patrimonial line!"

The men looked hesitantly at Naked Jaw.

"You four scout ahead," he said to a group standing nearest. "Two on each side of the path. Stop if you encounter anything strange and give the call of the red parrot."

The scouts disappeared up the narrow valley. There was no talk of blindfolds now. The men of the band traveled light. Most carried no more than a few weapons. The packs on their backs hung nearly empty. Only Twin Rabbit's two companions were heavily burdened.

After a few moments of shuffling about, the party set out. They had only been traveling a few seconds when a piercing whistle sounded from the thickets ahead.

"I hope these men aren't afraid of their shadows," grumbled Naked Jaw, but his face was worried as he pushed ahead of the group.

A racket of rustling branches reached their ears, accompanied by loud clapping sounds. A pair of buzzards blundered up through the underbrush and into the mists above, pumping their wings so hard the tips slapped against each other at the end of each down stroke. One of the scouts appeared on the path, holding up a hand in a gesture of caution. He pointed silently to the left, and Naked Jaw led them into the underbrush.

The body of a tapir lay on its side, just out of sight of the path. Its eye had been pecked out by the buzzards and the birds had begun to tear away at the wound in its side, the wound made by Naked Jaw's hunters. Ants swarmed over the stiffened carcass, so that in the dim light it almost seemed to be breathing. The stench of rotting meat hung in the air.

Naked Jaw walked up to the body, shoved it with his foot, and stared down at it, his forehead wrinkled as he concentrated. "Apparently the jaguars and monkeys who invaded our cave didn't care for their pickings," he remarked in a dry tone. "We'd best get started again."

Twin Rabbit made no comment. If the riddle of the abandoned tapir had any meaning to him, he did not show it.

"No time to be waiting here. We've got distance to cover," said Naked Jaw. "There will be better provender by midday."

He wants the men away from here, thought 8 Manik. He doesn't like them thinking about death and decay.

The men were willing enough to leave the foul smelling corpse, and soon the group was moving easily down the path, though Naked Jaw added two more to the screen of scouts in front and left a final pair to trail after the main party and guard against surprise attacks from the rear. A scramble up the hillside brought them to the path connecting Tikal to the cities to its west. Once on the main way, the line of men stretched out irregularly, their spirits rising as the path became easier. Naked Jaw made no attempt to organize them, allowing each to walk in whatever order he wished. The men moved with an unconscious swagger, a bold confidence absent from the solemn processions of the great cities or even the great victory parades in which captives were herded to the center of the city. Only Naked Jaw seemed to give any attention to their surroundings, sending runners forward to maintain contact with the scouts ranging ahead.

We will be to Double Cenote by midday, thought 8 Manik. He remembered the small cluster of compounds, no more than half a dozen. The path cut diagonally across a small plateau covered by alternating cornfields and patches of scrub where the land was being fallowed so that it could regenerate its fertility. As a trader he had often stopped to accept the hospitality at one or another of the households, never failing to leave the lineage head a gift in return. He far preferred to stop with the second largest clan in the village. The food they shared was always the best and the conversation pleasant and thoughtful as men sat in the dusk, idling away the hours before sleeping. If I can just get a chance to talk with Ground Sparrow in private, he thought, I can send word back to my sons. Of course, I wouldn't be surprised if he refused to speak to me at all, seeing me in this band of ruffians.

At the edge of the plateau, they caught up with the scouts who were standing in a group, just below a ridge lined with trees that screened the party from the village. "We saw nothing but a boy running toward the village," said one to Naked Jaw.

"Which means that you, yourselves, were seen," he replied sourly. "Why else would a father send his son away from the field in a rush at the middle of the day? The villagers are hiding their valuables at this moment. Well, let's get on in and see what we can find."

The band packed together in a loose clump and began to walk forward quickly. The path here was wide enough to allow two or three to walk abreast, so the group formed an irregular column advancing toward the cluster of compounds now clearly visible above the corn tassels. Nothing stirred in front of them; not a single farmer was to be seen tilling his fields as they made their way across the plateau. The hamlet looked deserted, as if the entire population had decided to migrate to the coast. The band shuffled to a halt and Naked Jaw stepped from among them. "Come out!" he shouted, "No one will be hurt if you deal with us."

8 Manik inspected Ground Sparrow's compound. Wisps of smoke rose from the hearth near the back and the pair of dogs within snarled at the intruders. Had the population simply run off, leaving all they could not carry to the mercy of the bandits? He edged toward the rear of the band, hoping to slip off for his private word with Ground Sparrow.

"We are poor people. We have nothing," a voice quavered from a compound behind 8 Manik. Glancing over his shoulder, he saw an old man standing in the doorway, facing Naked Jaw. Although his hair was thick, the mass of wrinkles on his face and the gaunt emaciated arms testified to the abundance of his years.

"No need to fear, Grandfather," boomed Naked Jaw amiably, using a term of affectionate respect. "We just need a few scraps of food and then we will pass on. We promise to pay you double its value when we return at the consummation of our journey."

"When the poor give to the rich, the Lords of Xibalba cackle with delight," said the old man. "We are few and have only enough to feed ourselves. How could we supply a company as large as yours?"

"Good fortune comes to those who feed a traveler on his way," said Naked Jaw. His voice contained an element of command, even as he repeated the maxim known to everyone in the Mayan lands.

8 Manik slipped behind the last of the bandits and ducked into the gateway of Ground Sparrow's compound. Despite the old man's words, Double Cenote was a relatively prosperous peasant village, but no peasant would willingly surrender part of his harvest for nothing more than the promise of future repayment.

"Turn him upside down and shake him," shouted one of the bandits. "You'll find that plenty will fall from his breechcloth."

"Tell his son we'll stick him on a post!" bellowed a second.

Naked Jaw threw his arm around the old man's shoulders. "Can't you see that Grandpa here is too old to have any seed left?" he said. "Why, his digging stick is so limp he hasn't planted a field in years."

The bandits guffawed with delight.

"Hunt around and find one of his granddaughters. We'll show him how it's done since it's been so long he probably can't remember." Naked Jaw continued. "After all, if we can't eat, we can still amuse ourselves with the only other thing worth doing in this place."

Faced with the threat of rape, the old man began to buckle. "Maybe we could find a few morsels," he conceded.

8 Manik had worked his way to the back of the crowd and ducked into the compound behind

them, hoping that no one would notice his departure. No sooner had he dodged in through the doorway than he found his arms pinned to his side and an obsidian blade at his throat.

"You come after my daughter and you die," hissed a voice in his ear.

"Ground Sparrow, it's me, 8 Manik," he squeaked.

A powerful arm twisted him around so that the owner of the house could stare into his face. Ground Sparrow's nose was only three inches from his own. 8 Manik saw the tension and hate in the familiar features turn, in an instant, to startled disbelief.

"Manik," Ground Sparrow blurted. "What are you doing with these ruffians?"

"Keep your voice down," hissed 8 Manik. "I've only been able to slip away for a minute."

"These men are thieves," whispered Ground Sparrow, restating the obvious in his excitement. "What is an honest man like you doing with this scum?"

A roar of laughter from outside made them turn to peek through the doorway. One of the bandits had dragged a teenage girl from the far compound and the men were pushing and prodding at her. Terrified, she was shuttled from one group to another, like a ball rebounding in the great game court. As she was pushed from one bunch of laughing men to the other, she crossed her arms ineffectually across her breasts to protect herself.

"They've kidnapped me," hissed 8 Manik, and in a few sentences tried to communicate his predicament to his old friend. Ground Sparrow's face filled with anxiety as the story tumbled out.

"What are you going to do?" he asked when 8 Manik stuttered to a halt.

"I don't know," answered 8 Manik. "The young lord's scheme is a mad one. A great leader like Pakal is always well guarded. My only hope is that I can escape once he is killed and make my way back to Tikal before the news of his death arrives. His concubine looked like a decent woman. I'm sure she won't do any harm to Hunapu unless one of his henchmen was there to make her. If you could get word to Ch'en, my wife, that I'm still alive."

Another roar came from outside. The old man's wife was dragging an immense pot used for making tamales out into the plaza, offering her most valuable item in an attempt to save the honor of her daughter. 8 Manik felt a twinge of pity for the innocence of the woman. Such an item, an heirloom perhaps, would mean nothing to the band of thieves.

"I can't be seen talking to you," said Ground Sparrow. "Go back and join them. I will try to get word to your wife. I sent my own daughters far into the field the minute the boy arrived telling of strangers. Maybe if I put all the food in our house outside my doorway, they will leave me alone.

8 Manik knew that to stay with Ground Sparrow would only bring reprisals against his friend. He whispered a few instructions for his sons and slipped back to join the increasingly boisterous crowd outside. He could only hope that Ground Sparrow believed his story and wasn't agreeing simply to avoid alienating a member of a bandit gang.

In the clearing between the compounds, the gathering had taken the air of a celebration. Two thirds of the group gathered around the pots of food that the old woman was dragging forward, squabbling in a friendly and eager manner over who had received the larger portions. A smaller cluster of men still crowded around the girl, but their mood had changed. The men were rivaling one another in professing their admiration for her beauty, praising each feature in increasingly elaborate compliments. Backed against the wall of her house, dazzled and confused, but also flattered by the attention, the girl stood with disheveled hair, her eyes darting from one speaker to another.

8 Manik wondered what she must be thinking. Life in a rural village was dull under the domination of parents and grandparents and the continued scrutiny of uncles, aunts, and cousins. These men with their swagger and boasting of valorous deeds and great wealth might offer a sense of romance to a girl whose best hope was that her husband would have enough land to feed her. The men were asking her to lead them out of the village to the site of the second cenote. Even she must realize that, once in the brush, they would be having their way with her.

The knot of men parted, for Twin Rabbit was advancing toward the girl. Taller than the rest, he moved with a stately elegance and reserve. Daunted, the thieves shuffled back until he stood alone before her, staring up and down her body with a frankness that made 8 Manik wince.

"You are lovely," Twin Rabbit intoned. "Too lovely for this bunch of ruffians." He barked a command over his shoulder and one of his heavy-laden servants rushed over to him. A brisk order was followed by hurried digging in the backpack, and the servant produced a robe of shimmering kingfisher feathers. Its iridescent plumage glittered in the rays of the sun that had battled its way through the afternoon clouds. Twin Rabbit swirled the cape and draped it over the young woman's shoulders. The girl began to giggle uncontrollably, fingering the soft folds with amazement.

"I'm going to take you with me," he announced, though it wasn't clear to 8 Manik whether he was promising her the cities of the world or merely that she would accompany him to a private spot. Awed, she followed him behind one of the house compounds.

A young member sneaked off to spy on them and came back with a grin on his face. "They're really going at it," he snickered. "She's lying on the cloak and he's pounding away like a rat in heat."

One of the bandits in the group began cursing under his breath. "I knew I was going to get her away for a poke. What does a great noble want with some peasant girl?"

"Same thing you want, Yellow Dog," said a friend. "But don't feel bad, you never had a chance anyway. With that scar on your face, you're too ugly."

"Women love my scar," retorted Yellow Dog. "It makes me look dangerous. There's no woman who can resist a rogue."

"I'm trying to remember a time when they didn't resist you," chimed in a third, good-naturedly. "Unless you mean that scrawny prostitute that couldn't resist any one of us."

Yellow Dog glowered at him. "What do we need this so-called lord for anyway?" he asked in a sullen tone. "From what I can see, he doesn't do any work and grabs the biggest part of everything we get for himself. If I wanted to live under the heel of an ahau, I'd still be working for that stingy potter I was apprenticed to in Bonampak. We'll do the fighting and dying and he'll swallow up the spoils."

"You're just mad because you're not getting any sex from that girl," said the friend, but 8 Manik had noticed a half dozen men nodding as Yellow Dog spat out his resentment of Twin Rabbit's condescension. For a second, he was tempted to chime in and fan the emotion of their resentment, but his cooler sense told him that in any disagreement, it would be the stranger who ended up getting blamed. The men shuffled back toward what was left of the food. Ground Sparrow had emerged from his compound with still more offerings and the men snatched at it eagerly. 8 Manik gave no indication of knowing the farmer and he saw that Ground Sparrow avoided his glance in return.

No sooner had the food been shared out than Naked Jaw began urging the men to pack up and move out. Moving from cluster to cluster in the open area, speaking jovially but with intensity, he kept stressing the same theme. Half the day is gone and we've hardly made any distance at all. 8 Manik assumed that he had some particular location where he wished to spend the night. The men around 8 Manik bolted their food and snatched up handfuls of tortillas to carry with them. In five minutes, they were standing in a single line in front of the lineage chief's compound.

"Grandfather, your hospitality has been wonderful," Naked Jaw announced in a large tone. "When we return, we will be glad to repay you for all we have taken. For now, accept this token of our gratitude."

He held out his hand and 8 Manik saw that he was offering a slab of jade, carved in the shape of a god holding an incense burner. The old man bowed, stunned to be offered a talisman of such great supernatural power. 8 Manik assumed that it must have been robbed from some traveling party of the priesthood. Just as the elder reached out to accept the gift, a scream sliced out of the compound behind him.

"My granddaughter! My granddaughter!" screamed the old woman. "Where is she? What have you done with her?"

The old man flinched and the jade dropped to the ground. Naked Jaw plunged down like a hawk dropping to its prey, snatching it from the earth and desperately shaking it to rid it of the contaminating soil. A gasp came from the crowd of men. No one could mistake the presaging of ill fortune that inevitably followed such treatment of a sacred object.

"You've got kids, grandma!" shouted a thief from the back who hadn't seen the jade fall. "Nothing happened she didn't enjoy. And you might get another present in nine moons or so!" He looked around; expecting the approval of the crowd, but consternation was everywhere. The men stared grimly at the ground at Naked Jaw's feet, as if by staring at the mark in the dust they could somehow erase the horrible omen.

"My granddaughter!" the old woman repeated again. "Who cares about pieces of jade? She was my prize!"

"Here she is," shouted another man, and Twin Rabbit reappeared, leading her by the arm. "Now shut your mouth and we'll be on our way!"

"My pet!" shouted the old woman, rushing to her. "Are you all right?" She cast a look of wicked resentment at Twin Rabbit. Her mood darkened. "What have you done?" she screamed at the girl and slapped her across the face.

The girl's hand leaped to her cheek, but she didn't make a sound, shrinking back against Twin Rabbit's side. The old woman's anger spent itself as quickly as it had come.

"Come inside, my darling," she cooed. "I'm sorry I hit you. I didn't know what I was doing."

"She's coming with me." Twin Rabbit's voice was calm.

"Are you possessed?" blurted Naked Jaw. "What raiding band travels with women? We're already late. She'll slow us down."

"It's quite simple, really," answered Twin Rabbit, his tone cool. "I might ask, what noble travels without a concubine? You agreed to that vendor's plan to enter Palenque as a delegation bringing gifts. For a noble to travel alone would be, shall we say, most frustrating."

"You beast!" The old woman flung herself at Twin Rabbit, seeking to scratch his eyes. An impetuous shove sent her sprawling back onto the dirt.

"Well, let's get going," conceded Naked Jaw. "We have a long way to travel and this won't make our journey any easier."

Incapacitated by rage and grief, the old woman lay in a heap on the floor of the plaza. The old man stooped to lift her up, but she pushed him angrily away. "My little one, my baby," she moaned.

Dispirited, their good humor evaporated by the stunning events of the past minutes, the bandits began to straggle from the village. Most were too amazed even to gossip among themselves. Towering above the shorter men, Twin Rabbit marched along, his arm around the girl's shoulders. What she thought of the departure, 8 Manik could not guess.

8 Manik joined the last stragglers to head down the path. He felt a firm grip on his arm and turned to see Naked Jaw walking beside him.

"Don't try to fall behind and drift away," said the leader. "You can't escape your fate that easily."

"Nor will you," snorted 8 Manik. "You have alienated the gods and men. This is a mad escapade and you will pay dearly for it in the end."

Naked Jaw didn't bother to argue. "True enough," he said in a grim tone, "but I will get through. I always have. And you will be there to help me."

8 Manik looked back one last time to the village. There, still huddled on the dust of the plaza, the peasant and his wife lay immobilized by their grief.

CHAPTER SIX

It was not until days later, after the band had forded the Usamacinta River, that Naked Jaw permitted a day of rest. On a raised bank above the river was a rough cluster of huts, probably used by peasants for shelter when they worked fields far from their homes. The huts were little more than a framework of poles supporting a thatched roof, but they did offer protection from the rains as long as the winds were not high. From the way that the lookouts trotted off without elaborate instructions, 8 Manik guessed that the band had stopped here in the past, seeking opportunities to swoop on trading parties when high water in the river disrupted their passage.

Even for a seasoned traveler like 8 Manik, the marches had been hard going. Naked Jaw only used the well-beaten trails when entering or leaving a village that he was bullying into offering supplies to the band. Once out of sight, he would send the group skidding down paths that were little more than traces in the forest. Sometimes their way led completely off trail to avoid dense areas of population. For two days their route had gone directly down the bed of a minor stream until the feet of the band were sodden and tender from continual immersion in the slimy waters. The detour around Mactum had taken the better part of two days to cover a distance 8 Manik could have traveled in three hours along the main path. For the men of the band, accustomed to brief, intense raids followed by periods of waiting, the long march was boring and debilitating. Grumbling increased daily.

8 Manik felt especially sorry for the girl. After the second night, Twin Rabbit tired of her and began offering her, first to his attendants, then to members of the band in order to curry favor with them. During the day she stumbled stolidly along the path, hardly seeming to notice torrential downpours that sent men scrambling for cover. She ate little of the food offered her and seemed to accept the role of camp follower without complaint. She was never separated from the feather cloak, clutching it in sun and rain even as it grew ever more ragged.

As evening fell and the men began to prepare a meager meal, he slipped over to the spot where she sat staring at the ground before her. She didn't move when he approached. He wasn't even sure she recognized his presence, so he reached out to touch her on the arm. She flinched away, then looked up at him with uncomprehending eyes.

"Is there anything I can do to help you?" he asked in a soft voice. The idea seemed idiotic as he said it. What could he do? At least I don't want her to feel she is alone, he thought.

"Don't touch me," she said. "It is forbidden for a commoner to have contact with a queen, wife of a great ahau."

"A queen?" 8 Manik was incredulous. It was obvious that a considerable number of men had done a great deal more than touch her in the last few days.

"He's going to make me his queen," she answered. "I will reign at Tikal by his side. The world will bow down to me." Her fingers gripped the edges of the feather cloak and pulled it even more tightly around her shoulders, even though the evening was steamy and the atmosphere felt dense around them.

8 Manik stifled an incredulous snort. He felt like her father, wanting to set her straight. "And these other men?" he asked, failing to keep an edge out of his voice.

"Maya lords have always shared their consorts," she replied serenely.

8 Manik thought of the aged figure of Jaguar Throne as he had seen her for years in the processions. Stalking along in magnificent isolation, she was able to terrorize priests with a single formidable glance. It was hard to imagine her being "shared," even by a lord as powerful as Shield Skull, her husband.

"They will bow before me," she repeated, "and I will bear him a son to rule after him."

"He has a son," retorted 8 Manik impatiently. "I have seen him. A fine child."

"Who could imagine the son of a concubine ruling the greatest city of all?" she remarked sarcastically.

8 Manik wondered how she would know whose son she was having, given the number of men with whom she had copulated. The son of some bandit climbing the pyramid steps and conversing with the gods? The thought was obscene. He bit back a caustic comment and turned away, only to confront Twin Rabbit, storming through the encampment, his eyes glittering with anger.

Twin Rabbit had not spoken to 8 Manik since the moment when Naked Jaw intervened to stop the sacrifice in the cave. Outwardly he affected to ignore the merchant, sometimes walking within inches from a spot where 8 Manik was sitting without swerving a hairsbreadth in his path. Still, on a half dozen occasions, 8 Manik had looked up to find the noble fixing him with a baleful, festering stare. 8 Manik realized that his existence humiliated Twin Rabbit, and the trader knew that nothing short of his death could erase the embarrassment of having been bested in front of a bunch of commoners.

"My lord," began 8 Manik with a humble gesture of deference, but the noble cut him off before he could speak further.

"Stay away from this woman," he snarled. "I will not have you defiling her."

"I never," 8 Manik began, but the noble continued in a rush.

"You must never touch this woman. If you so much as look in her direction, I will hang you in a tree and use you for target practice."

8 Manik felt anger flush within him and he found himself staring boldly, impudently, into the noble's eyes. Who was this man to question his motives? Did he think that 8 Manik was trying to seduce this innocent girl? "Unlike some," he spat, "I do not travel a road which so many others have taken before me."

"If I had my way," snapped Twin Rabbit. "You would not be traveling any one other than the path that leads to the realm of the dead. You had best enjoy each day as much as you can. Naked Jaw will not be able to protect you much longer."

"I can protect myself," said 8 Manik, speaking with more boldness than he felt. "Either in this world or on the paths of the dead. I do not need guards to protect me."

"We shall see soon enough," said Twin Rabbit, his tone softening and gaining an air of smug certainty. "Once we pass Chinikiha, we will be in the lands where Pakal is universally recognized as lord. It would be easy for one of his servants to hide beside the path and shoot a member of our party in the back. Since he would know the local byways better than any of the bandits, it would not be difficult for him to escape without a trace."

A simple plot, thought 8 Manik. But easily done. One of the bodyguards drops back, shoots, and suddenly rushes off in pursuit of a fictional henchman of Pakal. A fruitless chase ensues. The members of the bandit gang would be glad that it was 8 Manik and not one of them that had been killed, so Naked Jaw would be wise not to pursue the matter further.

"Accidents and ambushes can befall the great as well as the lowly," snapped 8 Manik, though he couldn't help feeling that his bluff was pretty unimpressive.

"Those who are favored by the gods suffer no accidents."

"But the moon is the most changeable of the gods," said 8 Manik. "Those who are the clients of the moon find that their fortunes wax and wane with it."

A look of shock flashed in Twin Rabbit's eyes. Apparently he had no recollection of the night when he had staggered forward in the cave to blurt out news of his trip to the moon. In an instant, his assurance had turned to wariness. He looked uncertain whether to pursue the conversation or break it off.

If he's smart, thought 8 Manik, he will stop right here. Any questions will reveal more than they discover.

"So you think that I am favored by the moon," said Twin Rabbit, his tone suddenly jocular. He even tilted his head to one side, as if the whole interaction had been nothing but a game. "What makes you think that? My name, perhaps?"

"No, O great ahau," said 8 Manik. "A man's name does not mark his fortune, only his past. I knew a man once whose mother insisted that he be named Star Alligator, because the Alligator God had appeared to her in a dream. He had told her, she said, that her son would never fail to turn a profit, as a trader and that he would travel far. As the family came from a guild of potters, his father objected strongly, but it was no use." 8 Manik allowed his voice to tail off as if the story were finished. The two of them stood facing one another in silence. You could almost hear Twin Rabbit arguing with himself. To ask for more information ("What happened to him?") would be to put himself in a position of a mendicant, as a beggar might ask for corn. He didn't care about the potter, but 8 Manik's use of the term star alligator suggested knowledge of his supernatural patron. Aggression against those favored by the gods was dangerous.

"Very well then," he said at last, trying to bluff his way out. "Just keep your distance, understand, and there won't be a problem."

"May you spend the night well," said 8 Manik, bowing extraordinarily low to affect deep reverence as he recited the traditional terms of politeness.

Twin Rabbit turned away, paused, turned back toward 8 Manik, stopped, and turned again and walked toward the shelter where the girl waited for him.

I wonder if that was a clever thing to do, thought 8 Manik. When the flush of anger had caused him to confront Twin Rabbit, 8 Manik had felt that he had nothing to lose. A man who is threatening you with death can hardly be alienated further. On the other hand, 8 Manik was sure that Twin Rabbit would have him watched even more closely in the future. It might have been better to have cringed away.

One advantage of being a trader, 8 Manik had found, was that you had to learn to let the past go. No one who bought and sold didn't, on some occasion, immediately realize that he had made a big mistake, that he could have purchased the same goods more cheaply or sold his stock at a higher price. What made these moments especially galling was the ill-concealed delight of the man who had bested you. 8 Manik had learned to walk away, not only physically by distancing himself from the other trader, but mentally by putting the event out of his mind. Now, not certain that he hadn't made a misstep by drawing Twin Rabbit's attention even more closely to himself, he walked to the far end of the cluster of huts and stared out into the tangle of jungle leading down a steep slope to the river below.

Through the leaves on the brush, he could see the glossy, dappled surface of the Usamacinta as it wound its way toward the gulf. The pace of the water was languid as it rippled around and over the trunks of trees that had been undermined by the erosion of the bank and toppled in. A mother duck and four ducklings had nested in the crook of one of the trees and were paddling industriously about in the eddy, ducking their heads beneath the surface in search of grubs and water beetles. Nothing else moved in the still afternoon air, but suddenly the ducklings abandoned their activities and huddled close to their mother. Her head jerked from side to side, nervously scanning upstream and down.

A branch stirred at 8 Manik's side. Naked Jaw had quietly walked up beside him. 8 Manik put a cautionary hand on the bandit leader's forearm to keep him from speaking.

"There's someone down there," he whispered, gesturing toward the river below.

"I don't see anything," Naked Jaw answered in a low tone. "I've got guards on the path upstream and down."

"Not on the path, in the river," said 8 Manik. He pointed with his lips toward the birds below. A V-shaped line of ripples was moving irregularly toward them. A reed, looking no different from the other rushes that lined the shore, made its way alongside the fallen trunk of the tree.

"I see it," whispered Naked Jaw. "A fowler."

The ripples worked their way toward the paddling birds, slowing to a stop just out of reach. The water calmed, so that the protruding hollow reed was just a point above the water's surface."

"Why doesn't he grab the birds while he can?" asked 8 Manik. "If he waits too long, he'll miss his chance."

"It's clear you never lived in the forest," said Naked Jaw. "If you reach out for any animal, they will flee. The trick is to get close, then let them come to you."

Even as they watched, the ducks began to venture from their huddle, resuming the peripatetic course they had followed before they sensed the disturbance in the water. The ducklings began to stray, and the mother began to nose about as well, following the course of the water skaters as they wandered across the surface. She stretched out her neck, took a pair of lazy strokes, and then vanished.

The hunter had grabbed the duck by her feet and jerked her beneath the surface. Somewhere in the murky, weed-choked water she must be thrashing wildly until the moment when he expertly snapped her neck. Only the slightest ripple showed on the surface to betray the death struggle below. The ducklings hardly seemed to notice their mother's disappearance.

A moment later, the head of the hunter broke from the water. An arm reached out over the trunk of a fallen tree and the man pulled himself up, naked and glistening in the dappled sunlight. In one hand he held the lifeless body of the duck; in the other, the woven belt with stone weights that he'd used to keep himself from floating to the surface. Sitting there on the tree, the youth reminded 8 Manik of Ix, his second son. They both had the same flattened face and strong, supple shoulders. The fowler lifted the duck to examine the quality of her plumage, his young face intent and pleasant as he ruffled the down on her breast.

A low whistle sounded upstream, like the cry of a nesting jungle bird, but if he heard it, the young man took no notice. The upstream guard was creeping down the path, looking for an open shot at the intruder. He had already fitted his spear into the hook at the end of his atlatl and was drawing back his arm. 8 Manik started to shout a warning to the fowler, but as he drew in his breath, Naked Jaw clapped a hand over his mouth. 8 Manik tried to rip the hand away but found himself as helpless as a child in the arms of a much larger bully. Within a second, the spear was thrown, catching the young man at the base of the throat and topping him backward through the foliage into the water. There was a brief flailing tumult, and the body lay still by the tangle of the bank. Finally, 8 Manik wrenched the hand away.

"You beast!" he screamed at Naked Jaw. "What did that boy do to you? He was just making his living."

"We travel in secret. If he had discovered our camp, we might be the dead ones, not him."

"Warn him! Threaten him! Ask him to join up with you! Give him a chance!" shouted 8 Manik, out of control. "Is that all you know how to do? Kill people?"

"It was him or the guard," said Naked Jaw, his voice placid and businesslike. "I could never permit a guard who didn't keep his post secure go on living. Soon the others would learn to be inattentive. That wasn't an easy shot, either."

"What's wrong with you?" 8 Manik spat out through clenched teeth, and he realized as he spoke that he meant not just Naked Jaw but the entire band. "That boy had no idea where we were. And how could the guard be expected to see under water? You do it because you are in love with death. You're drunk on it, as drunk as that idiot who shoves mushroom enemas up his butt."

"We're in the jungle," shrugged Naked Jaw. "Animals kill one another in the jungle. Would it be better if I sacrificed that young man on top of a pyramid in your beloved Tikal? There would be no shortage of people cheering me on then."

"But that is for a purpose," said 8 Manik, his words sounding weak in his own ears even as he said them. "We must propitiate the gods or the whole community will suffer."

"And thousands pack the plazas to watch the gods be served?" asked Naked Jaw. "You know that isn't true. They come because they take pleasure in seeing the prisoner dragged up the steps, desperate and afraid. Seeing his heart thrown, still beating, up toward the clouds. At least this young man didn't need to spend long nights waiting for his doom."

8 Manik stared at him in silence, sullen because of the truth of Naked Jaw's words. Although he was not one of those who slept in the plaza overnight to be certain of getting a good view of the ceremonies, curiosity had drawn him along with the rest to see the elaborately groomed priests escorting the victims to their doom. Who could deny that part of the thrill of the great ball games, which united ritual and sport in a grand display, was the knowledge that the loser must forfeit his life? All life was a great battle, and the actions of men were just one small part of the greater war.

"I still would have given him a chance," he muttered and turned away. Naked Jaw did not pursue him. 8 Manik made his stolid way back to the spot where he'd dropped his pack. The men of the camp were lounging about great fires, tired but looking forward to a day of rest, jovially heckling the pair roasting a tapir for the evening meal. Night was falling quickly and a shower in the afternoon had cleared the sky of clouds. The grumbling of the long march had given way to a rising sense of expectation. 8 Manik wondered how much the men knew of this plan to raid the second city of the Mayan world. He suspected that they would follow Naked Jaw anywhere, so confident were they in his leadership. A pair motioned for him to join them, but he turned away and flopped on the ground alone.

He was overwhelmed by the sense that he had betrayed the young man by pointing him out to Naked Jaw. He knew that this made no sense, that the guard was already tracking the boy down without help from anyone on the bank. Even if 8 Manik had shouted a warning, he told himself, the young man would only have had time to look up in amazement before he was slaughtered. If anything, the warning would have accelerated the attack, not delayed it even for a second. No matter what he told himself, the sense of guilt persisted.

The image of the youth flashed though his mind over and over again. The face so happy and self satisfied with the exercise of his hunting skill. The easy, confident grace with which he sat on the tree trunk cut short in an instant. If I had thrown a stone at the duck to startle it to sudden flight, the young man might have moved on safely under water. The breathing reed would never have provided enough of a target and he might not have been seen until he had crossed to the far bank. Everything would have been different. But it wasn't different. The boy was dead and no one cared. Most of all, he resented Naked Jaw's "that wasn't an easy shot." The young man became nothing more than an incident of marksmanship, appraised by a cool judge of the fine art of killing.

The boy looked like Ix. Where was Ix now? He must have made contact with Muan and the two of them would have searched Tikal compound to compound. What had happened to the message he had sent back from the peasant village? Would they have tried to follow him? Traveling straight along the main paths with no need for concealment and lightly burdened, they could actually be ahead of the bandits by now. Muan was older than Ix, and always calmer, but with his son missing and wife and mother in hysterics, who knew what he would do? "Two boys are less than one," his father liked to say, "Because each will urge the other to do what they both know they shouldn't." They could be anywhere. Could they have found the trail? They could be killed tonight, trying to save him.

All through the swift tropical dusk and into the night, the worries raced through 8 Manik's mind, becoming more and more intense. He rolled on his back and stared up through the trees, trying to quell the panic that was taking control. His sons might seem young, but they were men, full grown. It was useless to try to guess what they might be doing. They might have decided to split up, sending one toward Palenque and leaving the other to protect their mother and Kayab. Maybe they had found little Hunapu, either helped by some informant or by simple chance. Hope flared and died within him, leaving a sickening sense of despair behind. If all he had left was grasping at such chances as these, he was in a sorry situation indeed. He closed his eyes and tried to force himself to sleep, but the snores of the band around him and the ideas pounding inside his skull made sleep impossible.

Through a small gap in the canopy above, he could see the half moon riding in a sky now completely free of clouds. People said that sleeping in the moonlight would drive a man insane. Perhaps Twin Rabbit with his belief that the rabbit in the moon was his animal double had fallen under the power of the moon. Like the moon, he had no constant character and rushed from one idea to another, from terrified anger to expansive confidence to craven doubt. As the moon waxed to full, he would also grow bolder and more uncontrolled. In seven days, the moon would be full. That must be the moment he had chosen to strike, for Pakal's ceremonies of renewal must be timed to the full moon as well. Back in the cave he had raged at Naked Jaw about being short of time. Now, with the goal in sight, they had called this day of rest. It must be the moon that was setting the schedule.

Manik felt he had run into a blank wall. Palenque would be packed for the ceremonies. Lords from the surrounding communities over which Pakal held sway would be en route in a few days, bringing with them retinues of loyal retainers. Of all times for a bandit gang to strike, this must surely be the worst. Forty men might overawe a village and steal its food and women, but it was ludicrous to think of them facing down a mob. There had been raids on minor centers before, but they were hit and run affairs, often timed to the harvest when many urban dwellers traveled to visit rural relatives and help with work in the fields.

He's mad, 8 Manik thought to himself, but as these words formed in his mind, he still felt unsatisfied. Twin Rabbit might be beguiled by the moon or drunk on power and drugs, but Naked Jaw was not the sort of adventurer to fall prey to wild schemes. He must know something that 8 Manik didn't which made him think that there was a reasonable chance of success. Either Twin Rabbit had some hold over the bandit leader, which 8 Manik could not comprehend, or Twin Rabbit was possessed of some divinely given power to persuade him.

The camp was asleep. The dying fire glowed a dull red, barely illuminating the faces of the men nearby, but most had taken shelter in the huts. There was a curious, peaceful quality to the faces of the men at rest. They looked like children who had drowsed off to sleep as their elders discussed some problem that didn't concern them. By days, these men worked hard at looking intimidating. They liked to daub black clay below their eyes to make themselves look more threatening. The gentle glow from the embers stripped away the bravado, leaving men who were neither victim nor murderer. They looked, 8 Manik thought, like that dead boy who floated in the river.

Maybe Naked Jaw was right. Here in the forest, one killed to survive. The delight of the youth ruffling the feathers of the bird he had killed was paralleled by the pride of Naked Jaw in the guard's perfectly thrown spear. 8 Manik had traveled for most of his life, but he found himself in a world as strange to him as that of the gods in the sky or the nine layers of Xibalba below.

Something balked in 8 Manik's practical mind. The boy had been doing nothing wrong. Although his trade as a feather merchant never settled to the mundane level of dealing in common duck feathers, 8 Manik felt a special affinity for fowlers. Their work, like his, took them far from their families. In the evenings, they loved to tell tales boasting of their craft in stalking and the chances of the hunt. The fer-de-lance, most poisonous of all snakes, was their special patron, taking the same prey as they did and living in same environment. Many a fowler had died alone after being bitten by one of these snakes. Now this boy had fallen to a predator far more cruel and unfeeling.

8 Manik's thoughts turned to Ix, who loved to bathe in the placid rivers that ran through the countryside. While other traders flopped in the shade, too exhausted even to swat away the ever-present mosquitoes, Ix would immerse himself up in a nearby stream and lie on his back, staring up through the break in the treetops at the sky above. Often fishermen worked the streams, putting in fish traps or preparing a drive to shallow waters where companions would spear the stranded prey. Ix would work alongside them, asking no reward other than the pleasure of splashing in the sunlit waters and participating in the excitement of the hunt. Later he would stride confidently back into camp, his wet body shining, carrying a fish from the catch which the fishing party had awarded him in thanks for his assistance.

8 Manik's hip began to ache from the pressure of the ground, so he rolled over, searching in vain for a more comfortable spot in the rocky soil. The thought of the dead boy's body, abandoned in the backwater along the bank, tortured him. A man could not go unprepared on the ways that led to a battle with the lords of Xibalba. There were parts of the underworld where souls found rest and repose, but those who failed in battle were tortured unmercifully. Great lords descended to the underworld from tombs stacked with food, weapons, and valuables with which to win the cooperation of the denizens of the lower world. Often several servants were included to assist them in their passage. Even the poorest peasant would be buried with a jade bead in his mouth for

supernatural protection. The young fisherman whose possessions surely lay where he stripped them off before entering the water would be helpless before the rapacious lords of death.

8 Manik rolled over again. The camp was silent. With the setting of the moon, the camp had become encased in darkness. He reached out for the net bag he carried on his back and fumbled inside until his hand touched the stone knife blade he had secreted there. Not jade. Not a bead. But something to give the fowler on his journey.

"You're a fool," he said to himself, his lips moving in the dark. "If the guards don't hear you and spear you, you'll step on a poisonous snake and join the fisherman on the road to death."

He held the blade, barely three inches long, in front of his face, but the dark was so intense that he caught no gleam from the angles of its obsidian surface. He let his finger rub across the clean struck edges. Sharp enough, he thought, to slash an exposed wrist or throat and bring a life to its end. Uncoiling from the ground until he was standing upright, he began a slow journey across the clearing. Each footfall required a gentle preliminary testing to make sure no snapping twig would betray him.

When he reached the edge of the clearing, he realized that he was standing next to the hut where Twin Rabbit slept. He could hear the big man's heavy breathing and the lighter sound of the girl's respiration. The two of them and their servants would be packed together under the crude thatched roof. If he could see in the dark, thought 8 Manik, one quick slash would put this madness to rest. But what if he killed one of the servants or the girl? He struggled to penetrate the gloom without success.

Would it make any difference if he killed a servant or the girl by mistake? He would only have time for a stroke or two before the rest were awake and on top of him. Twin Rabbit would sacrifice him, but by now 8 Manik was certain that he would die anyway. Hunapu was as doomed as he was. The boy might well be dead already. Twin Rabbit could easily have left instructions to have the boy done away with as soon as their expedition was out of sight. But the woman had said that she would care for the boy. She hadn't looked as if she were lying.

It seemed to 8 Manik as if the entire universe had shuddered and was watching him as he crouched by the shanty, waiting for his decision. Even the mosquitoes had stopped whining about his ears. Great cycles of time, stretching back thousands of years and onward for another thousand, were hanging on this moment. He could strike blindly and take a life at random. If his fate were to send Twin Rabbit on the paths of the dead, then the blow would land true. The lord was everything no Mayan man should be – selfish, dangerous, and insane. Time itself may have picked 8 Manik for this moment. There would not be another opportunity.

"Where salt falls upon the ground, nothing can grow," the god had told him in his dream. "I water the ground with my blood." Had the god been warning him against this moment, or choosing him for it? And if fate turned here, what of the boy in the river? He also had a journey to take. He deserved his chance, slim as it might be, to defeat the lords of the underworld and make his way back to earth.

Shaking himself like a dog spraying water from its fur, 8 Manik turned from the hut and crept through the underbrush to the riverbank. He didn't even pause at the top of the steep slope, but slid through the underbrush until his toes dug in the mud of the river bottom and the waters of the Usamacinta lapped against his knees. His descent had sounded like a tapir crashing through the underbrush, but no sounds of alarm reached him from above. Perhaps the guards were sleeping as soundly as Twin Rabbit.

Heedless of the noise, he splashed his way to the tree trunk and felt on the far side. The boy's body was there, floating face down. Fumbling in the darkness, 8 Manik turned the corpse, pried open the jaws, and forced the blade between the jaws, rigid with death. He was glad that he couldn't see the young man he was helping. He didn't think he could have confronted those staring eyes by moonlight. With a convulsive thrust, 8 Manik pushed the body outward into the center of the river and felt the current pull it away on its journey into the underworld.

CHAPTER SEVEN

8 Manik slept late, awaking at mid-morning to find the rest of the camp slowly making its way to action. A quarter of the bandits were still asleep and men who seemed in no hurry to either cook or eat were just fanning the fires into flame. Insects droned indifferently through the air of the clearing, swerving only to avoid the dense clouds of smoke rising from the damp firewood. An easy indolence seemed to have captured the entire band as they lazily shook off the fatigue of the long marches behind them. Feeling strangely at ease, 8 Manik looked up through the spangled sunlight of the forest canopy above and watched a hummingbird hover not five feet above his head, drinking the nectar of a flowering vine.

The memory of Twin Rabbit's threats from the day before tore into 8 Manik's sense of peace. Gently, without giving the appearance of haste, he rolled on his side to glance furtively at the hut on the edge of the clearing. Neither of Twin Rabbit's servants was in sight. This must mean that Twin Rabbit was gone, because one of them was always present wherever the noble went. Still trying to give an impression of casual disinterest,

8 Manik's gaze swept the camp. His survey confirmed that Twin Rabbit had left the camp. I'd rather know where he was, thought 8 Manik, than wonder what he might be up to. For the noble to rise early was unusual and must mean that whatever errand he was on was of great importance.

Naked Jaw was nowhere in sight either. His absence might explain the casual atmosphere in the camp. Although Naked Jaw was no order-shouting tyrant, when he was present the men took pains to appear industrious. Because there was no clear second-in-command, any time Naked Jaw left the group, activity staggered to a halt.

8 Manik wondered why Naked Jaw was so reluctant to share his power. The men of the band accepted his direction, even when Naked Jaw was pushing the pace the hardest. His manner with the men was always easy and confident, but even so, 8 Manik decided, the leader must fear that having an assistant would mean he had a rival.

Satisfied Twin Rabbit's servants had left the camp with him, 8 Manik rolled on his back, propping his head up on the folded net bag. The familiar, friendly lump made by the knife blade was absent. Even though he knew it would have proved of little use in any real fight, the thought that he had a weapon that others didn't know existed had consoled 8 Manik throughout the journey. For a moment he wondered whether he should have lashed out at Twin Rabbit the night before, but he banished the idea before it reached the level of regret. Time to move on, he thought, and take his chances as they came.

There was a roar of laughter from the bushes on the far side of the camp, and one of the brigands came swaggering into the clearing, adjusting his loincloth as he strode, an insolent smirk on his face. "Best trip I've ever been on," he announced to the camp in general. "We should bring a princess along every time. Who's next?"

A young lad, probably not more than fifteen, attempted to edge inconspicuously toward the edge of the forest. His shyness drew forth catcalls from the men around the fire. "I'll come along and show you how to do it!" "Let gramps get in ahead of you! He can't keep it up for very long!" "He can't get it up at all. You'll be waiting all day." The boy sped toward the bushes as quickly as he could, prompting more laughter from the group. "We'll see him again in two minutes," shouted one. "These young guys can't wait for anything."

8 Manik moved to sit next to the bandit the others called grandpa. The wrinkles on his face were a testament to his advancing years, though his hair was as black as a raven's plumage and he walked at a pace that matched any of the younger men. "Boys," said 8 Manik, "They like to talk about it as much as they enjoy doing it."

The older man held out a tortilla wrapped around a roasted piece of tapir's flesh and nodded amiably. "Just like old men," he replied.

"You must be the oldest one here," said 8 Manik politely. Age brought respect and referring to another's advancing years was always a welcome pleasantry.

"No so much older than you," the man replied, matching courtesy for courtesy, even though he probably was at least a dozen years older than 8 Manik.

8 Manik took a bite from the food that the man had proffered and chewed slowly. Mixing eating with talking was seldom done among the poorer folk, and the old man let 8 Manik chew the tough meat without interruption. He would remain still until 8 Manik felt prepared to speak. 8 Manik's head was full of questions, but to quiz too directly was not polite.

"Not many as old as you and me on this journey," 8 Manik said at last.

"True. Being a bandit is a young man's station in life," the old man agreed, smiling and displaying a gap-toothed grin.

The question hung in the between them. Why are you here? What is an old man doing, traveling with a band of thieves?

"Have you been a member of this band long?" asked 8 Manik. "Naked Jaw is one of the most renowned bandits in the lowlands, but his name has only come to my ears in the last few years."

"I'm an apprentice in this trade, as you are," said Grandpa. "It hasn't been three years since I was a peasant, tilling the corn fields and fearing the arrival of bands like this one. Ours wasn't the largest lineage in the village, but had land enough to win the respect of our neighbors. Our village was safer than most since it was less than a day from Palenque and few bandits chose to risk the wrath of Pakal the Great by raiding so close to his center of power. When new construction levies were announced, we bore our share of the work without complaint. When the gods instructed our betters to go to war, we answered the call. For me, there wasn't much risk for I was never foolish enough to rush to the front of the army in search of glory or booty."

"We older ones are more valued for our counsel than our fighting capacity," said 8 Manik.

"There weren't that many wars," said Grandpa. "Few states care to deny Pakal the Great what he demands. They say he is favored by the gods."

"His name is great though all of the cities I have ever visited," said 8 Manik, wondering when the story would return to the explanation of why the old man was one of the bandits.

"That was the problem," said the old man. "What Pakal demanded, not even the proudest lord dared to refuse. There are few nobles so brave that they believe they can prevail in the great game when bound and drugged into submission."

8 Manik nodded. When a city met defeat in battle and its lord was captured alive, he would be dragged by his hair before the triumphant leader. Naked and humiliated, he could beg for his life. Some "merciful" lords would spare the lives of their foes, forcing them to live on in captivity, even for years.

More often, the loser was offered the "chance" of playing the sacred ball game for his life. Exhausted, he faced the champion chosen by his captors, usually a man far younger and more skilled than he. It was said that a dominant lord might ensure against an incredibly lucky shot by drugging and further harassing his old foe. For the crowd eagerly awaiting the demise of their enemy, the sight of seeing him stagger about the ball court was especially pleasing, giving them the pleasure of more taunts and abuse.

Once the winning point was scored, the vanquished leader was bound up, as a symbolic recreation of the ball itself, and hurled from the parapet of the ball court again and again until he died. Humiliating as the spectacle was, there were few who refused the offer. The alternative, sacrifice in the temple, while quicker and less painful, meant eternal death, for no one could survive the journey through the underworld without a heart in his body.

"Without foes," the old man went on, "the number of sacrificial victims grew small and the gods grew bored. Pakal dominated all the northern cities and Palenque was rich as it had never been before, but the city dwellers missed their amusements of earlier years.

"The men of a city love to boast of its celebrations," said 8 Manik, just to keep the conversation going. He glanced over at the old man and saw his mouth turned downward, the lips compressed together. The eyes stared, unblinking, as if he were focusing on something far away or some time far in the past.

The old man's voice was growing bitter. "People without celebrations grow bored with their leaders. Even as they take the gifts of tribute from other cities which he collects and distributes to his followers, they mutter about how much greater they would be with a younger man, with fresher blood to water the soil."

"Everything grows old," agreed 8 Manik. "Even the love of a man for his lord."

"Two years ago," said the old man, "it fell upon the leader of our village to wait upon the great Pakal. None of the great lord's kinsmen would bring him the cup at the start of the ceremony, as is usually the custom when the sun ahau comes to water the soil with his own blood and restore its power. This year it would be Celestial Bird himself, the man who had inherited the office as head of the dominant clan not two years before."

"Strange," said 8 Manik, wondering when this tale would return to the subject of why an old man found himself in a bandit camp. Perhaps his mind was wandering off, as the thoughts of the elderly will.

"Strange and wonderful," the voice went on, betraying little hint of emotion. "When Pakal had come five years before, he had been surrounded by his nobles. We caught only a glimpse of him. No one saw the blood dripping on the ground from his self-sacrifice. Now one of us would be in the inner circle. You can imagine how excited we were, and how proudly Celestial Bird walked among us."

"When the lord arrived in his sedan chair, he was surrounded by the greatest procession we had ever seen. Fifty members of his closest kin, arrayed for battle. They wore headdresses with magnificent quetzal plumes and textiles of the finest hues. It was a day like no other in the memory of the village. The lord walked to the center of the village and Celestial Bird rushed forward with a cup to relieve his thirst after the journey. In his eagerness, Celestial Bird tripped and the contents of the cup sprayed on Lord Pakal himself!"

"How humiliating," said 8 Manik. "What an embarrassing accident."

"Not an accident," corrected the old man. "A rebellion. Pakal withdrew at once. No ceremony was held. That was bad enough. Two days later, Pakal's younger son, Kan Xul, appeared in the plaza of Palenque to denounce us. We had committed an act of desecration, assaulted our rightful lord. We must be punished."

"For spilling a drink on his garments?" 8 Manik was incredulous.

"We were terrified when we heard the rumors. Most of us didn't believe them. Then we heard that Chan Bahlum, Pakal's oldest son, was gathering an army to conquer our so-called rebellion. We gathered that night to decide what to do. Some absolutely refused to leave their fields; others counseled flight. No one, not one person, suggested resistance against our divine lords.

"My wife and I wept bitterly, but we decided to go with those who were fleeing to the east. What else could we do? We packed as much food as we could, gathered our two sons and three daughters, the youngest was only nine, and prepared to leave at dawn.

"The sun was just beginning to turn the horizon pink when we started out, but we should have fled the night before. We had just reached the edge of the village when the army stormed out of the cornfields, dressed as if they were facing a great city in battle. My wife screamed, but one of the warriors plunged his spear in her neck to silence her. Then there was screaming everywhere. They smashed children with their long war clubs. I tried to fight, but what chance did I have against veterans of battle? The same one who had killed my wife clubbed me on the side of the head with his spear, knocking me unconscious.

"When I regained consciousness, the line of raiders was moving through the village, taking prisoners. I crawled under my wife and son and lay there, pretending to be dead."

"Terrible," said 8 Manik.

"What else could I do?" asked the old man, perhaps misunderstanding 8 Manik's expression of sympathy for a criticism. "I was terrified and defeated. I had done my best to protect my family, and I had been useless. I could hear the raiding party routing the villagers from their houses and driving them off toward Palenque. The women and children were screaming and the men were trying to argue, desperately insisting that they had always been loyal to the great lord.

"By noon they were gone and the village was quiet. No, the village was gone entirely, for what is a village but the people in it? I didn't dare to move for fear that one of the raiders would come back to the village looking for booty. It was only after nightfall that I made my way to the forest."

8 Manik struggled to think of some phrase that might express his sympathy. The fear of armed attack had never been part of his life growing up in Tikal. Over a century before, when Tikal suffered defeat at the hands of Caracol, the great battle had occurred far from the city. Old people relayed stories of the triumphant entry of Lord Water, kalomte of Caracol, into Tikal. Their parents had seen the steles and altars being smashed, the record of Tikal's proud ancestry erased. The tales were tragic but brought no sense of personal danger.

"When the moon rose that night and I finally summoned the courage to stand up," the old man went on, "everything was still. Two dozen of us lay dead; the rest had been taken away. My wife and children lay at my feet and her blood was crusted on my body. It cracked and crumbled with every move I made. I had spent the day being silent and now I found I could not weep. I just stood there, a useless coward. A wild dog came out of the forest and began to feed on one of the corpses, but I didn't have the energy to drive him away."

"At least her death was sudden," said 8 Manik.

"Yes, there was that," said the old man bitterly. "Some of the bodies had lain for hours in the hot sun, groaning for a drink of water. Calling for friends and relatives who had been taken away, or who might be lying dead next to them and they didn't know it. I had been a friend to many of them, but I had preferred to lie there feigning death to even making a trip to the well to carry them a cup of water."

"I'm sure I would have been terrified as well," said 8 Manik, but something in the back of his mind made him want to draw away from the old man. How could he have waited all day before he moved? "Perhaps the blow knocked part of your soul out of your head. It would have returned with the setting sun."

A roar of laughter from the men in the camp interrupted them. The youth had returned from the shadows of the forest, looking enormously pleased with himself.

"Did she tell you that you were the biggest man she'd ever seen?" bellowed one of the other men. "That's what she told me!"

"And me! And me!" chorused several others, but their derision did nothing to dim the look of smug satisfaction on the youth's face.

The old man stared at the hubbub, but his eyes seemed to be looking right through it. "That night I washed myself in the stream. All my family, with the exception of my sister, was gone. She had married a stone carver from Palenque, and we visited regularly. Without thinking about it, I wandered into the city and found myself at her house the following night. She greeted me with tears of joy, but when I started to tell my story, she shushed me and pushed me back into their house. The news of the great rebellion was all over the city. It was embarrassing enough that she had been born in the rebel village. If she were caught harboring me, she and her family would be traitors too."

"She turned you away?"   8 Manik was stunned that the bonds of kinship should be so betrayed.

"No, she hid me. She never said anything, but it was clear that I was a danger to her. When I said I was leaving the city, she urged me to stay, but she did not beg too long or too hard."

"And then?" prompted 8 Manik.

"There was to be a great ball game in which the leader of our village, the same young man who had 'assaulted' the Lord Pakal, would play for his life against a champion chosen from the city. Everyone was rushing to see the procession. The nobles were in their finery, the poorer folk just hoping for a glimpse of the game. In the excitement it was easy for me to drift along with the mob, one face among many. If I had left at night, someone might have wondered where I was going and take notice. This time all were intent on the spectacle to come.

"The crowd carried me along. I didn't really care where I was going. My only thought was to avoid bringing danger to my sister. Then, just as the crowd approached the main plaza, I saw the people from my village. They were tied around the arms and chest and legs, shuffling along with their eyes downcast. Some wept, some pleaded for mercy, but most were as numb as I, unable to comprehend what had happened to them."

"It's true," murmured 8 Manik. "Most of the sacrificial victims make no resistance. They just walk along in the direction indicated."

"I was terrified that they would look up and recognize me," said the old man. "I wasn't afraid they would betray me. I don't think I would have minded being taken with them; I was in such a state.

The thought that they would know that I had seen their shame, all naked and abused, was humiliating to me."

"Did anyone from your village look up and recognize you?" asked 8 Manik.

"No! They just shuffled to their fate. Once they were past me, I felt free to go, as if some cord around me had been cut. By dusk, I was far from Palenque. I never want to see the place again. Two days later a couple of young men from this band ambushed me on the road. They were most disappointed that I had nothing to steal. One said he might as well take my sandals, but I offered to throw myself in as part of the bargain. Naked Jaw was amused at the transaction, so here I am."

"So now you are a killer too." 8 Manik was surprised that the thought had slipped through his lips.

"I don't kill anyone," said the old man, without seeming defensive. "Most of what the band gets is through intimidation. As for the band members, they are men not unlike the people in my old village. Most are younger sons from families that could not afford to keep them or apprentices who ran away from craftsmen who abused them. A few are men who answered a call for battle and found they like the thrill of combat. There is no place for them in the city or countryside, so they make a living the best way they know how."

"Maybe you are right," said 8 Manik, but he didn't mean it. It was hard to accept the idea of a band of thieves being ordinary and hard-working people like himself. The memory of the young fowler's body pitching into the river was too recent for him to accept the idea of banditry as a trade like any other.

"I'm glad that we have come to rest here, near the river," said the old man. "The rumors are flying that Pakal is preparing to celebrate a great anniversary of his lifetime. Many travelers will be heading along this path and we will find easy pickings from those who can afford to lose the valuables we take."

"You think that we are stopping here?" asked 8 Manik.

"That's what all the men say. They say that we camped here for several months three years ago until the lords raised an army to evict us. The river is a fine place for ambush, and you can flee upstream or down leaving no traces if things get too dangerous."

"But we're not stopping here," blurted 8 Manik. "Twin Rabbit means to go all of the way to Palenque. He told me that himself before my journey started."

The effect of this statement on the old man was startling. It was as if an evil wind had struck him. He slumped to one side, and then fell heavily onto the ground. He lay there, gasping and stuttering incoherently. His eyes rolled upward so that only the whites were visible. The noise of his fall attracted the attention of one of the men who were chattering together.

"Look what's happening to gramps," he shouted, jumping to his feet and rushing over.

"Stand back!" shouted 8 Manik. "Give his soul room!"

The man jumped back. Like all the Maya, he knew that when a piece of the soul was knocked free of the body, it simply fell to the ground, invisible. An incautious person might tread on it and destroy it. An even more dangerous possibility was that the soul fragment would enter the wrong body and live there, at war with the body's rightful soul dweller. The other men joined in a circle at a safe distance from the old man.

Like a grandmother comforting an infant, 8 Manik made a series of sweeping gestures with his arms, herding any wayward parts of the soul back toward the body where they belonged. He crooned softly to comfort them and guide them in their return. The words were simple, like those of a mother rocking a baby. The old man convulsed again, then his body relaxed. A trickle of blood ran from the corner of his mouth. He had bitten his tongue during the seizure. His eyes slowly rolled back forward and his shook his head to try to order his thoughts.

"What did you see, gramps?" asked the youth.

"Darkness," muttered the old man. "Moving down, down, and then turning back. The stairway was steep. There wasn't a single star in the sky. But there was light ahead and below me."

"A dark staircase," repeated the youth. "What does that mean?"

"Hush," said 8 Manik. "Let him talk." He put an arm under the old man's back and lifted him until he was sitting on the ground, his legs stretched out in front of him. The men were crouched around him, the circle narrowing as they pressed in, eager to hear about the vision.

"What did you see," persisted one who was leaning over 8 Manik's shoulder.

"Nothing," muttered the old man. "A dark journey. A flash of light."

"Death!" said another. "It's the journey into the underworld. The trip we all must take to battle the lords of Xibalba. You're going to die before this trip is done, old man. That's what the ancestors are telling you."

"This man shall not die!" came the voice of Twin Rabbit, towering over the huddled men. They looked up at him in awe. He was dressed in the fine woven garments, which only nobles had the right to wear. On his head was the tall plumed battle helmet of a great lord. His left arm carried the flint shield, which identified him as the lord of a great city-state. With his right hand, he gripped a magnificent spear. It had a shaft made of polished mahogany with plumes dangling from the huge obsidian point hafted to the tip. Bathed in the noonday sunlight that fell into the clearing, he was every inch a man born to rule. Behind him stood his servants, adorned only slightly less magnificently than he. The three stood in a phalanx, dominating the sun-splattered clearing.

The old man, his jaw still slack with a long strand of spittle handing from his lower lip, looked up into the face of Twin Rabbit.

"This man shall not die," repeated Twin Rabbit, and held his spear aloft. He has had a vision of darkness, but the route he has seen is not the journey of death, but of life! His vision began in darkness and traveled down, the first stage of rebirth. Just as the maize seed travels deep into the earth, and then bursts upward to crack the soil and climb to the sun, so his vision begins in darkness but turn to light. If this merchant had left him undisturbed, if he had allowed his communication with the gods to continue, the old man would have foreseen the end of the journey as well as the beginning."

The men's heads swiveled toward 8 Manik and he could feel their anger welling up against him. Messages from the gods were rare and valuable. Who was he to frustrate, and possibly anger, those who ruled their lives? Stunned by the turn of events, 8 Manik struggled to justify himself.

"He was an old man in trouble. I was only trying to make him comfortable." His words sounded empty as he heard himself stuttering them out.

Twin Rabbit was glorying in his moment of advantage. "The messages of the gods come to us infrequently," he thundered, "and they are always sent for a purpose. Those who displease the gods bring ill fortune not only on themselves but on all around them."

The men around 8 Manik flinched back, as if he would contaminate them with his sins. 8 Manik could see where Twin Rabbit was headed. Sinners were a threat to those around them. The gods were angry and could only be appeased through sacrifice. Who better to sacrifice than the one who could bring trouble upon the whole band?

Twin Rabbit stood impassive and aloof, gazing directly into 8 Manik's eyes.

What is he waiting for? wondered 8 Manik. Why doesn't he simply announce that I must die? It's my own fault. I had the chance to kill him last night and didn't. Furious at himself, he glared back into the face of the figure above him. Still the noble remained motionless. The eyes flickered. Twin Rabbit was waiting for something to happen. For just a second, uncertainty flittered in his gaze.

He's waiting for me to crawl. In a flash, 8 Manik could see the carvings on the monuments back in Tikal. The great kalomtes of the city stood in their feathered array. Before them were their prisoners, stripped naked, dragged by their hair to confront their fate. To be a great lord, you must be able to daunt both your followers and your enemies. To be a great lord, you must display to your followers the power you have to command and intimidate lesser mortals, people like themselves.

To his amazement, 8 Manik realized that he wasn't afraid of Twin Rabbit. He wasn't even sorry that he hadn't stabbed him the night before. For all his plumes and projects, this man was no greater than the fowler who had been killed at the river, no more important than little Hunapu, wherever this madman might have taken him. I will not crouch and look up at this man, he thought.

Slowly 8 Manik stood up, never breaking the invisible bond that held his eyes to those of Twin Rabbit, staring at him across the seated body of the old man. Seething with fury, 8 Manik wanted to throw himself at Twin Rabbit, to tear the battle helmet from his head and throw it to the ground, but he knew that if he did, it would break the spell that held everyone in the clearing motionless. In the eyes that stared back, he saw a fury no less intense than his own. He realized that Twin Rabbit must act now with power and restraint, a lord whose powers over life and death ensured the safety of the band.

Twin Rabbit raised his spear, then held it slanting across his body in the formal posture of condemnation. When he spoke, his voice did not quiver or fail.

"Prepare the merchant for sacrifice," he announced. "Once he has died and I have bathed my feet in his blood, I will hear and announce the remainder of this message from the gods."

CHAPTER EIGHT

8 Manik felt his body grow numb as the words of condemnation were spoken. A cold feeling swept up his legs, surging toward his brain. His heart pounded in his chest. He could feel the blood draining from his cheeks. Intently, he willed his knees to lock and hold his legs straight so that he would not collapse on the ground. Twin Rabbit reached toward his waistband, preparing to draw the sacrificial knife of Stormy Sky.

"I cannot fall at his feet," 8 Manik muttered to himself. "I refuse to give him the moment of triumph."

A hoarse scream rang out in the clearing. 8 Manik and Twin Rabbit both startled at the same moment. The old man at was writhing at their feet, his arms flailing, and guttural sounds escaped between his clenched teeth.

Without thinking, 8 Manik stooped once again to gather the old man in his arms, but as he bent forward, his skull cracked against Twin Rabbit's forehead, for the noble also was drawn to the old man. The two of them recoiled. 8 Manik lost his balance and thumped to a clumsy position on his seat. Twin Rabbit had fallen to his hands and knees and scrambled forward like a baby in pursuit of a toy.

"Speak!" he ordered, grabbing the old man by his shoulders and shaking him. "Speak!"

A long rattling sound rang through the clearing. Spit sprayed in Twin Rabbit's face. He didn't pause to wipe it off.

"Speak!" he shouted, his face inches from the old man's trembling lips. The body thrashed and the old man's left arm clouted Twin Rabbit on the ear. The noble drew back, paused, and delivered a resounding slap on the old man's cheek. The old man's legs pounded the ground, kicking up clouds of dust into the still air.

Twin Rabbit grabbed the old man's shoulders. "Speak to me now!" he repeated. He his face was fixed in a grimace of eagerness, so that for a moment it looked as if the rigor of death had overcome his body. The two bodies twisted on the ground as the old man flailed about. Twin Rabbit's head snapped forward so that the chin of the old man was beside his ear. To 8 Manik's amazement, the eyes that stared at him across Twin Rabbit's shoulder had not rolled back. The old man give 8 Manik a squint of recognition, then his body went limp.

"Is he dead?" asked one of the bandits as the whole band clustered round to witness the scene.

"No," said Twin Rabbit, "he will return to consciousness and when he does he will carry a message from the gods." As he spoke, the body of the man stirred and his eyelids fluttered. The noble bent over him so close that his lips almost brushed the old man's nose. "What did you see?" he asked.

"There will be four who climb the mountain," said the old man, his tone flat and his voice drowsy.

"Four who climb," echoed Twin Rabbit, his voice hoarse with reverence.

"There must be four and only four," the old man repeated. "First will come the rabbit, then comes death, then comes the deer, then..."

"Then? Then?" parroted Twin Rabbit.

"The one I could not see. The one who carries infinity in his hands."

"The mountain? What mountain will they climb?" Twin Rabbit was intent.

"Above the River Otolum the mountain rises," the old man's voice had fallen into a singsong chant. "By day it is red, but when the moon shines, all is white. Within….beneath…. the old lord falls….four and only four must go…The Rabbit, Death, the Deer, and the Other." His face looked directly up into Twin Rabbit's eyes. "When that journey is done, you will have taken Pakal's place in Palenque!"

"The gods have spoken. You have heard it, all of you," shouted Twin Rabbit.

8 Manik shook his head, wondering what it could mean. He had been to Palenque. It backed up to a range of hills next to the Otolum River, but there was nothing that anyone would call a mountain nearby. The hills, covered with lush forest, were green, not red. The gods spoke in riddles, as far as he could see.

"The mountain which rises beside the Otolum is the pyramid raised by Pakal," said Twin Rabbit. "Every pyramid is a mountain, made to the greater glory of the gods. The steps which the old man referred to are the great entrance to the temple or mountain top which only those chosen by the gods may climb."

The men looked at him reverently.

"The four are the four who will climb the steps. Each represents one of the cardinal points of the world, while the mountain is the fifth direction, the center. At the center of this world we will gain the power to defeat the Lord Pakal. The gods themselves have spoken it."

"We heard it," said a member of the crowd. "We heard it ourselves." The men around nodded in agreement.

Naked Jaw stepped into the circle and turned to face them, standing with his back to Twin Rabbit in a blatant affront to his dignity. He's jealous of the power that Twin Rabbit has over them, thought 8 Manik. He's afraid that the noble will take his band from him, but he can't contradict what the gods have spoken.

"The gods have spoken," Naked Jaw shouted, "Four will go to the mountain top. The rabbit is this proud noble that you see before you. Death is none other than myself. My name, Naked Jaw, is a reference to the fiercest lord of Xibalba, whose flesh has fallen away from his skeleton. The deer is this man we have brought along with us. Manik means deer and he was born on 8 Manik, the day of good fortune and success in travel. Fortunate indeed for us, for no one else has that name, even though the name is common enough in our lands.

"The gods have spoken!" moaned the old man from the ground.

"The gods have spoken!" shouted the men of the band.

8 Manik heard Twin Rabbit's breath hiss inward through his teeth as he strived to mask his frustration. "And the other?" he asked, sarcasm dripping from his lips as he launched the question.

"The other is not of this world," answered Naked Jaw, turning to him. "That is why the gods do not name it. But it will be with us. It could even be," he added with a calculating look in his eye, "your own nagual, come to protect you as you climb the mountain."

Twin Rabbit rose to his feet. The two leaders stood facing one another, each eyeing the other with loathing and disgust. 8 Manik could feel the rivalry crackling between them, like the air when a thunderstorm is about to burst over the forest. The bandits, who had pressed in so eagerly to hear the prophesy, fell silent, as if caught in a spell they didn't understand. The old man stirred in the dust beside 8 Manik.

"How fortunate we are," he said, his voice quavering, "to have two great leaders such as these." His voice gained strength as he spoke. "How lucky a band we are, to be led by those who are ordained to ascend close to heaven to commune with the gods themselves!"

The men began to cheer wildly, shouting that Naked Jaw and Twin Rabbit were the greatest leaders in the entire world. Twin Rabbit looked nonplused, but Naked Jaw raised his arms to accept the accolades of the group, then embraced first one and then another of the men. He addressed each by name, stopping to remind one about a wound he had received in a raid two years before and to tease two brothers about whether the younger was giving the older the deference he was due.

Twin Rabbit stood proud and aloof. No noble would ever tolerate such familiarity with those below him in society. His lips worked nervously, but he forced them into an uneven smile. Naked Jaw turned in the crowd of men and shot a triumphant glance back over his shoulder, as if he were saying aloud, "What ever made you think you could steal them from me?" In response, Twin Rabbit turned and stalked to the hut. Something moved in the shadow under the thatched roof. The girl was waiting there for him.

"It seems that the gods have saved my life," 8 Manik said to the old man. The two of them were still crouched on the dirt of the clearing.

"No, I am the one who saved your life," the old man replied in a matter of fact tone.

"Your vision was a fake?" asked 8 Manik. He had seen the seers and fortunetellers who worked in the markets. They would writhe on the ground as soon as any peasant paid them and produce marvelous prophesies of danger or great wealth. No one who asked was ever going to live a life of boredom or routine. 8 Manik felt the most amazing thing about such shamans was that anyone was foolish enough to believe them.

The old man's vision had been different. 8 Manik had heard the teeth grinding as the man's jaws clenched together, felt the rigid thrusting of his arms and legs. It couldn't have been staged; it was too intense and sudden.

"The first part was real enough," said the old man. "The dark journey, the stairs that turn back. I saw those as clearly as I am seeing you now."

"And the rest?" asked 8 Manik.

"I served my village as a shaman ever since I was a boy and started having visions," said the old man. "I soon learned that no one is satisfied with what the gods provide. Many times there is no vision at all, just an attack. People want everything neat and explicit, as if the shaman was a child sent to market to buy four ears of corn, a measure of salt, and a chili. They want to know what everything means.

"Of course," said 8 Manik. "When the ahau goes to the top of the pyramid to take intoxicating herbs or mushrooms, he always comes back with a message."

"And so do I," said the man. "When I saw that Twin Rabbit wanted to sacrifice you, I just threw in the business about the deer to make you indispensable. If you were in a vision of his success, he couldn't kill you."

"But don't people get angry with you when your visions prove false?" asked 8 Manik. "I mean the fortune tellers in the markets move from place to place. No one can confront them if their stories don't come true. You lived in a small village where everyone knew you for a lifetime. Didn't the other villagers become disillusioned when things you predicted actually didn't happen?"

"Just the reverse," said the old man. He paused to lift himself to his feet and brush the dust from his arms and legs. "They blamed themselves when what I told them didn't come to pass. They thought they misunderstood me. They were proud to have such a powerful seer in their village. It made them feel safe and protected." The old man's face darkened with concern. "And then I failed them. If I were a real man of vision, I would have saved them. The gods have turned their wrath upon me."

"It was the warriors who killed your people," said 8 Manik. "It was the leaders who sent them."

"Why didn't I warn our headman to be more careful with the libation he brought to the great Pakal? I didn't see even enough to tell the people to leave the village immediately. I am to blame for the slaughter in the village. If I had been all I claimed to be, they all would have survived." The old man was staring into the shadows of the forest, his shoulders slumped in grief.

"You couldn't..." 8 Manik began, but he bit back the words. He had been about to say that there was no way that the old man could have known what was going to happen when he realized that that was exactly what the old man thought he should have known. "No one knows the secrets in the hearts of men," he tried. "Not even the gods. If the gods of Tikal had known of Caracol's plans, they would have protected Tikal and their temples would not have been defaced. Isn't that why great ahaus wear mirrors on their chests? It deflects the evil of rivals' souls back on them, even when the evil doer himself is unaware of his intentions."

The old man looked at 8 Manik and shook his head. "It is kind of you to say these things," he said, "but you cannot know what it is to have even the slightest insight into the world of the gods. I am an imperfect and common vessel, but there is another world far more glorious than we can imagine. It is perfect and whole. The planets dance in the sky in accordance with its laws and everything on earth is shaped by its power."

The old man turned and walked toward the river, his steps loaded with the grief of his failure, his inability to protect those he loved. 8 Manik looked after him, puzzled. How could a man both boast of having faked his visions and yet have such belief in his power? How could he blame himself for what Pakal had done, as if slaughtering one's own people were the most natural, the most predictable, action that one could anticipate? It made no sense.

With a shudder, 8 Manik thought of his own efforts to protect little Hunapu. He felt that Twin Rabbit's concubine would protect the child, but how could he trust his sense of her character? She might want to save the boy but give way quickly when confronted by one of Twin Rabbit's ruffians. 8 Manik was certain that the affront to Pakal had been no accident. The headman had been tripped to create a cause for the subsequent raid. Why else would Pakal have broken with tradition and have the lowest official serve him with an honor reserved for his nearest and most trusted kinsmen? If nobles could so deliberately murder their most loyal followers, who could trust the intentions of anyone?

This morning, when he had awakened, 8 Manik had felt relaxed and at ease. He hadn't looked in amazement for the roof of his own home and felt the shock of his predicament coming back to them. He had lain and watched the sun filter through the trees. The ground had felt natural under his shoulder blades.

I'm becoming one of them, he thought with a shudder. Last night I stood outside Twin Rabbit's hut and planned to kill him with no more repugnance that if I were going to wring the neck of a turkey. I raged at Naked Jaw over the killing of the boy in the stream, and not hours later I was holding a life in my hand and weighing its chances as if I were deciding whether to invest in a particular load of feathers in the market. If I had slashed in the dark and murdered one of his bodyguards, or even the girl, by mistake, I would only have cared that I missed Twin Rabbit. If I could have been certain that my blow would land true, I would not have hesitated for a second.

A macaw flew across the clearing; its plumage flashed as the spattered sunlight and shade glistened on the feathers of its wings. 8 Manik marveled in the smooth curve of its flight. Ch'en had always said macaws were harbingers of good fortune. 8 Manik thought it ironic, for he had never turned a profit when dealing in macaw feathers in all the years he had been trading. Still, he never saw one without the childish sense than something wonderful was about to happen.

The branches at the side of the clearing rustled and three blindfolded men were led into camp. Each had an enormous bundle on his back, huge textile bags which bulged in every direction but which, in 8 Manik's opinion, were not terribly heavy because the men who carried them walked with an easy grace. One of Twin Rabbit's bodyguards was leading them with a rope that was tied from waist to waist. In the center of the clearing the first stumbled and fell heavily to one side, dragging the other two down with them as the rope that connected them snapped taut.

The bandits who had drifted away after the prophecy came larking back into the clearing like children on the day of a great festival. It had been a day of many wonders. First there was the luscious easy morning, then the visions of the old man, and they responded to this new event as if it were an amusement arranged solely for their entertainment. They jostled each other to get closer to the men with the loads, pointing and laughing as the blindfolded carriers struggled to get to their feet. One of the bandits fashioned a lasso out of a vine and set it at the feet of one blindfolded porter. The man shifted his weight from one foot to another, stepping now on one side of the snare that he could not see and then on the other, but by chance neither of his feet fell into the trap. The men laughed as the game continued and a few called out to the carrier, trying to get him to step within the loop.

Before they could accomplish this prank, Twin Rabbit came out of his hut and walked to the center of the group. Striding to the largest of the men, he tore the blindfold from his eyes. With the covering taken from the man's face, 8 Manik saw that his skin was wrinkled and old.

"I am sorry, Old Kawil," Twin Rabbit boomed. "These men have treated you badly, but they will soon see that they owe you thanks for all you have brought."

Old Kawil dropped to his knees and put his forehead on the tips of Twin Rabbit's toes. "My Lord," he said, "I have brought all that you commanded."

"This man was the steward of the household when I was a lad," Twin Rabbit announced. "It was he, more than my nursemaid, who followed me about the palace, comforting me when I fell, teaching the patterns of etiquette and speech which are fitting to men of my station. He is the man who was a mother to me. Henceforth, he shall be called 'ahau-mother,' the lord mother of the kingdom we are about to create."

8 Manik wondered how the men who had recently been harassing Old Kawil would take this strange announcement, but before anyone could respond, Twin Rabbit raised his voice and continued. "From this day onward, no man in this band will ever skulk about in the shadows. We will march into Palenque as the proud lords that we are, dressed as the retinue of a great lord must. Even if your mothers meet us on the way, they will not recognize you because they will be dazzled by the glory of your passage."

He bent and ripped open the bundle that Old Kawil had been carrying, spilling out the contents on the dirt of the clearing. Colors as brilliant as the plumage of the most flamboyant jungle bird blazed in the sunlight. The fabric of these textiles was cotton, like that of the loincloth of the humblest bandit, but these dyed and embroidered fabrics were worthy of the finest noble. The iridescent feathers of jungle birds shimmered on the fabrics. Twin Rabbit strode to the second bundle and then the third, dumping their invaluable contents into a great heap. The men looked on, awestruck.

"Come, find raiment that is that is worthy of you," cried Twin Rabbit with a grandiloquent wave of his arm.

The men, released like a group of children allowed by their parents to run play with their fellows, rushed to paw through the luxuries before them. In one pile they found embroidered loincloths and great capes and, in the second, bracelets, anklets, headdresses, nose plugs, and ear spools of jade and obsidian. The third bag was stuffed with elaborate sandals that laced up the calf; belts adorned with jade and hematite, and long feathered wands to be carried to fan a great lord or lady. Within minutes the men were prancing through the clearing with the costumes they had assembled.

Naked Jaw stood in the shadows of the forest, looking on with undisguised disdain, his arms crossed in front of his chest. A cynical smile curved across his lips, and he glanced toward Twin Rabbit as if to say, "nice move."

The two of them reminded 8 Manik of the players he had seen in the ball court at Tikal. As the solid rubber ball had flown back and forth from one end of the court to the other, each of the proud players had become more and more extreme in his play, spinning into each move with increasing abandon. Neither would retreat a single step and the cries of the audience spurred them to more and more spectacular efforts. That game had ended unexpectedly when one of the contestants had tripped and slammed full tilt into the sloping wall of the embankment, snapping his neck. Now Naked Jaw's glittered with the same fierce intensity that 8 Manik had seen so many years before. Neither of these men would quit until one of them was dead.

For the moment, Twin Rabbit held the advantage, and after letting the men parade their finery, he began to attend to the details of their dress. This stole is never worn with the loose end visible to the side, he told one. The feathers of this quetzal headdress must always curve down from a horizontal placement. Sandals are laced to the rear when approaching a great lord, but at other times it is permissible for the laces to be tied to the front. Such distinctions sounded like gibberish to 8 Manik, but the men listened attentively and hastened to make their costumes conform to the rules.

"Tomorrow," said Twin Rabbit. "We will deal with the details of body painting! For today, I wish to present the consort without whom no lord could ever travel. With a flourish, he pointed to the hut and the girl appeared, dressed like the wife of a great lord. Her skirt was completely covered with rippling patterns of blue or green, her breast covered by a folded cloth of red. Her cheeks were daubed with pale blue paint; her hair was braided around her head like a halo.

"The color of sacrifice," muttered 8 Manik. "Only a priest should wear blue colored paint in public."

"A priest or a victim," answered the old man who stood beside him, "I wonder if she knows?"

The girl toddled forward in her unfamiliar sandals and the men parted on both sides as she walked toward Twin Rabbit. He stretched his arm out toward her and stood motionless and elegant as she approached. Where the men parted, an aisle had formed between them, and as she passed, they involuntarily dipped their heads in deference.

"Not two hours ago these men were rolling in the leaves with her," whispered 8 Manik. "Now they treat her like a lady ahau."

"My lord," she said to Twin Rabbit, and bowed her head to touch his feet the way that Old Kawil had done. 8 Manik guessed she had been coached for this moment. She rose with an awkward gesture and turned to stand beside Twin Rabbit, facing the men. She looked up at him in admiration, seeming to delight in each grand gesture he made.

"Tomorrow," he shouted, "we begin our procession to Palenque. It will be the greatest adventure in the history of man! When we have completed our task, you will all be lords of the land and I will have assumed my rightful place as the leader of the greatest city of the world. These clothes may look fine to you today, but I tell you, before this month is out, you will regard them as the rags of a humble peasant!"

The bodyguards shouted their approval. The men joined in somewhat raggedly, perhaps because many had started their lives as peasants. A brief frown passed across Twin Rabbit's face, but he forged on with his speech.

"Those whom the gods love live in no fear of danger. Those whom the gods favor are willing to risk any chance. As a young man in these very jungles, I proved my manhood by strangling a jaguar with my bare hands. In two days, I will strangle the butcher Pakal on the highest temple of Palenque, that dark usurper who followed his mother's footsteps to the throne and replaced the legitimate line of kingship which must run through men only."

The bandits stirred uneasily. Twin Rabbit's claim to nobility might be impressive, but this insistence on bloodlines didn't strike a chord in their experience, 8 Manik thought. Twin Rabbit seemed to sense their disinterest, for he returned to his intoxicating promises of wealth.

"Pakal is nothing but a bandit who has stolen an entire city. He is an imposter who has no greater right to its wealth than you. His storehouses are stuffed with jewelry, textiles, and all kinds of precious things. That wealth shall be ours!"

Again the bodyguards cheered, and the men joined in more quickly this time.

"Pakal's palace is filled with a harem of gorgeous young women, eager to satisfy his every demand. After tomorrow night, that harem will belong to you!"

This time the cheering was enthusiastic.

"The gods themselves have decreed that Pakal must die. You heard it this very day. Together we will turn the world upside down! Tomorrow we begin a journey in the sunlight that will carry us to the pinnacle of greatness!"

The men cheered again. Twin Rabbit took the girl on his arm and strode back to his hut. When he reached it, he turned, gave a broad wave of his arm and disappeared into the shadows within.

"We won't see him again until tomorrow,"

said the old man. "It would spoil the effect if he reappeared. Every procession, every vision for that matter, must come to a definite end or it loses its power."

"I doubt we'd ever see him again if Naked Jaw had his way," said 8 Manik, pointing toward the far side of the clearing. Naked Jaw was still standing in the spot he occupied when the speech had begun. The men around him were chatting with one another and moving away, but he had not flinched. His hatred for Twin Rabbit was evident, intensified like a liquid that has almost boiled away at the bottom of a pot.

Maybe Naked Jaw will kill him tonight, thought 8 Manik. If I could get as close as I did last night, I'm sure Naked Jaw will do better. And he will have a few of his band that would do whatever he asked to help him. For a moment, 8 Manik toyed with talking to Naked Jaw and putting him up to the task, but he rejected the idea as infeasible. Naked Jaw would take whatever action he wanted, regardless of what 8 Manik might say. If he did kill Twin Rabbit, would Hunapu be safer or more in danger? Surely there would be some allies left in Tikal who would be eager to lash out in revenge. Twin Rabbit must live if Hunapu were to survive.

Coming full circle, 8 Manik wondered if he shouldn't sleep near Twin Rabbit's hut so he might raise an alarm should any harm come that way. This idea seemed as insane as the first. Could he become a guard dog at the door ready to sacrifice itself for his master?

The jungle is the world of death, thought 8 Manik. Yesterday I witnessed the end of the fowler and I was repulsed. This afternoon I weigh the chance of life and death for a man I hate, valuing his existence by the opportunities it opens for me. If I march with Twin Rabbit, I'm marching to my doom. If Naked Jaw kills him here, Hunapu will surely die. Twin Rabbit wants to sacrifice me, but I find I must try to keep him alive.

For a few minutes, despair swept over 8 Manik and he struggled to catch his breath. The whole effort was pointless. Naked Jaw, Twin Rabbit, and Pakal were each, in his own way, great lords who sacrificed the lives of others without compunction. 8 Manik was a feather merchant, a husband, a father, which was all he had ever wanted to be. These men spent their lives working for the greater glory of their kingdoms and themselves. How could he hope to match wits with them?

Yet even in his despair, 8 Manik knew he would not give up. Twin Rabbit would spend the night inside the hut, unable to emerge for fear of diminishing the grand exit he had made. Naked Jaw would stalk the clearing, hoping for an opportunity to reclaim the unquestioning loyalty of his men. The Lord Pakal would dream the night away in the great palace of Palenque, not knowing that a child he had raised was returning, intent on his destruction. And 8 Manik, feather merchant, would stay alive, looking for the opportunity to escape the game of death into which he had been flung.

CHAPTER NINE

The next morning, Twin Rabbit was up before dawn and by the time the men awoke, he was standing in the middle of the clearing with a half dozen paint pots and brushes clustered at his feet. Looking around, he called one of the older men to him and began to apply red paint to his cheeks and chin.   At first the man began to squirm at the ticklish sensation of the brush, but when Twin Rabbit spoke to him sharply, he submitted as humbly as a child to its first haircut.

"We enter Palenque as warriors of a great kingdom, so you must look like one," said Twin Rabbit, sounding like a mother admonishing her son. "The red has to come back to the tip of the earlobe, and then we'll put black on the forehead and the chest. You have to stand very still for a half hour until it dries. You don't want to get it on your cloak. It will never come out."

The other men crowded around, curious and Xexcited.

"I'm painting him as a leader of one hundred men," explained Twin Rabbit. "See how the stripes on the forehead run vertically, indicating authority. This one," he added, pointing to a young man jostling his elbow, "will be a leader of twenty and the stripes will be horizontal."   The "leader of twenty" looked visibly disappointed but perked up when the next three attained only simple soldier status.

"Look at them," the old man whispered in 8 Manik's ear. "It's nothing but ochre dug from the earth and daubed on their faces, but you would think that it had made them into heroes and great captains on the field of battle."

"You don't have to tell a feather merchant about the power of decoration," 8 Manik answered. "From the greatest ahau to the lowest courtesan, everyone puts on his clothes when he meets the world."

"Or takes them off, if it is a courtesan," said the old man. "Look at Naked Jaw, frowning with disapproval. I'll bet that Twin Rabbit doesn't get any paint on him."

One glance at the bandit leader confirmed what the old man had said. His body was rigid and his eyes darted from side to side as if he were searching for some means of escape. To 8 Manik, his dilemma seemed obvious. To refuse to participate when Twin Rabbit was giving the men the pretensions to status they craved would isolate him from his followers. He would seem to be belittling them at the moment when they were feeling the best about themselves. To go forward and allow himself to be painted would put him in the control of his rival. No wonder he hung back, playing for time.

"I need twenty soldiers and two slaves, not counting my guards," announced Twin Rabbit. "To travel with a larger group would place an excessive burden on one's host. To travel with a smaller group would not be commensurate with my rank."

The remaining men pushed forward, eager to be included. Twin Rabbit lined them up in order of height. The tallest and shortest he pulled from the line, leaving a corps of men roughly equal in stature. Disappointed, the others wandered back to the fire. The old man accepted his rejection with relief. Clearly he had no desire to return to Palenque.

Only two men and the youngest of the bandits remained when Naked Jaw made his move. Striding boldly to the bodyguard who was holding a great frond to shade Twin Rabbit, he seized it from him and held it aloft. "I shall go disguised as a slave," he announced. "I will carry the sunshade of the great lord of Naj Tunich and stand behind him in the procession."

The men looked baffled at this announcement. One was pushed out in front, looking diffident but needing to speak. "But you are our captain. How can you go disguised as a slave? It would dishonor us all."

Naked Jaw walked over and clapped him on the shoulder. "You and I have been together for many years, and I know the love you bear for me. If I were to go in the procession adorned in finery, I would attract attention. Who knows how many people have seen me over the years? No one looks at a slave. It is the way that is best."

And keeps him standing behind Twin Rabbit so that he can knife him if there is any treachery, thought 8 Manik.

"The leader of the band may go in whatever form he desires," said Twin Rabbit over his shoulder. It was almost as if he were giving permission. Naked Jaw stiffened, but maintained his control.

"Now for you," continued Twin Rabbit, turning to the boy. "You will be at my side with your hand on my arm."

The boy's face brightened.

You will be my concubine. No great noble travels only with his wife. A single woman of high and noble birth could never be expected to satisfy his desires. Your cheeks are soft and your figure is slight. With a little padding, you would make a shapely maiden indeed.

The men looking on roared with laughter. The boy's face fell and he started to pull away from Twin Rabbit, but the surrounding crowd pushed him back.

"Yesterday he's rolling around in the bushes; today, someone else is on top!" one yelled.

"Oh, lover girl, give yourself to me," shouted a second.

"No, I won't do it," said the boy, his cheeks blushing with embarrassment.

"You will!" said Twin Rabbit, grabbing the boy by the wrist. "You will if I have to tie you down to paint you."

The boy continued struggling, but Naked Jaw stepped forward. "Listen," he said, looking straight into the young man's eyes, "everyone has to do his part. Do you think I like walking about as a slave? We do what we have to do in order to survive."

His words seemed to have a hypnotic effect on the boy. Looking straight into Naked Jaw's eyes, he stopped struggling. Finally he whimpered, "but the men will laugh at me."

"No one will laugh at you."

"They will."

Naked Jaw turned to the surrounding men. "If any of you wants to laugh at this young man when he is in costume, you are free to do so. You will also be free to find out what it is like to meet me in single combat when this adventure is done. Now, does anyone feel inclined to tease this boy?"

The men shuffled and looked at their feet.

"Maybe it would be better if you all promised me that you wouldn't tease him. Then we will know that we understand each other. Well?"

The men mumbled promises not to tease and backed away. Still, there were more than a few resentful glances as they left.

"Get on with your painting," said Naked Jaw to Twin Rabbit. For the moment, he was the one giving orders again.

By noon, the band was assembled and ready to move out. 8 Manik, unpainted, stood with one of Twin Rabbit's bodyguards. He thinks I might try to make a break for freedom as we enter the city, thought 8 Manik, so he has assigned a bodyguard to keep me under control. Immediately to his right, Naked Jaw stood, his feather sunshade cradled in the crook of his arm as he waited for Twin Rabbit to finish setting the order of march.

As he stood in the clearing, 8 Manik thought that it made sense that Twin Rabbit was so insistent that he not escape. When Twin Rabbit abandoned his original plan of disguising the band as a group of merchants, he immediately wanted to eliminate 8 Manik who, if he escaped, could warn the leaders of Palenque of the threatened coup. What was hard to understand were Naked Jaw's efforts to keep him alive. Surely 8 Manik's knowledge was just as great a danger to the bandit leader. Naked Jaw was not a man to engage in wild schemes. His style was to make sharp raids against small groups, like isolated villages or bands of merchants. Naked Jaw would lose as much as Twin Rabbit by betrayal.

Betrayal. The word hung in 8 Manik's mind like the echoes of a great drum in the still air. Naked Jaw could not simply arrange to have Twin Rabbit killed, for death did not end the power of a man or object. As a child of the ruling lines of Tikal and Palenque, Twin Rabbit was possessor of enormous supernatural power, power that had to be destroyed upon his death. Even objects like pots or sculptured heads that were buried with a corpse were "killed" by drilling a hole in them to release their vital power. A statue or portrait was killed by slashing the forehead and left eye. Dead or alive, Twin Rabbit would not lose his power to work mischief if not properly handled, so Naked Jaw must be careful not to offend the gods by openly betraying the noble.

Betrayal. Twin Rabbit was turning on his foster father, seeking to use an outlaw band to advance the interests of his native city, Tikal, against the city that had nurtured him. Betrayal. In a sense, Naked Jaw was betraying the trust that the men of his band had in him. He could be sure of success on jungle paths and help them evade whatever punitive expeditions might be sent against them. In Palenque, Naked Jaw was exposing them to certain annihilation. Maybe he was keeping 8 Manik alive to serve as a guide to escape the city if things went wrong. Maybe Naked Jaw knew where Hunapu was being held and could promise to help release him if Manik 8 could aid in his escape.

"You've been standing there thinking for some time." Naked Jaw's confident voice startled him. "What are you thinking about? Looking for an opportunity to bolt? That's what Twin Rabbit says you'll do. I wouldn't advise it. His bodyguards will cut you down before you take three steps.

"I was just wondering," said 8 Manik in a level tone, trying to appear as if they were chatting about nothing more important than the weather, "what I am doing here. I seem to be a danger to everyone and a help to no one. Yet, I am alive."

"The will of the gods," shrugged Naked Jaw. "What are any of us doing here?"

"You can't fool me with that kind of talk," said 8 Manik. "You always know what you are doing, or at least you think you do."

Naked Jaw's sardonic glance swept away from the head of the procession where two "leaders of twenty" were arguing over who had the right to walk first in the procession. He looked directly into 8 Manik's eyes. "I know what I am trying to do," he said. "No man knows for certain what he is doing."

"What makes me so valuable?" 8 Manik began, but Naked Jaw hushed him with a gesture. Twin Rabbit was moving to take up his position just in front of them. He wore a long, spotless, white cape, and when he turned toward them, the reflection from the hematite mirror hanging on his chest glared in the sun, almost blinded them. Hanging around his neck was a necklace of spondylus shells. The great woven loincloth around his hips was held in place by a leather belt studded with jade disks. Hanging from the belt was a jade mask, carved in the likeness of Itzamna, the reptile god. 8 Manik had to admit that he looked a man of innate and overwhelming nobility.

With a flourish, Twin Rabbit turned to the front of the line. On either side stood the girl from the village and the boy in concubine's clothing, both looking exceedingly uncomfortable.

"You must remember to move with the slow measured tread of a confident warrior," announced Twin Rabbit. "A man of power is never in a hurry. He knows that nothing important can happen until he arrives. Only the common folk rush about from one place to another. We are less than a thousand paces from the main road to Palenque. Until then, you may move separately through the forest, but when the group reforms along the road everyone must stay in position."

The men started out moving slowly and there was little inclination to accelerate their pace. They must be wondering, 8 Manik thought, whether this elaborate deception would work. Until someone defers to them, they will not really believe that it can succeed.

Within half an hour, they reached the path. Twin Rabbit sent a scout ahead to make certain that no one would witness them emerging from the forest, and they waited until the way was clear. Once he had them in the bright sunshine of the open path, he paused for one last set of instructions to his impostors.

"A warrior walks with his eyes straight ahead. He never turns to the side or displays the slightest interest in what he might see. His thoughts are on greater matters than the huts of farmers or the fields of peasants. He holds himself tall. He looks at the world through half lidded eyes. Nothing interests him because nothing is superior to him except his lord, the person to whom he dedicates his undivided attention. When he speaks to a superior he always uses the term "ak" or "lord." When you address me, you will use the term "ahau."

The men arranged themselves in order. Looking suitably grave, they began their slow progress down the path. On the slope of the next hill was a small village. Figures could be seen moving through the fields, hurrying back to the households clustered along the road. The men of the band closed ranks and slowed their self-conscious pace even further as they approached.

"Let's see what lords of the land we are," whispered Naked Jaw to 8 Manik.

One of the villagers hurried forward, holding out a cup of hospitality in front of his face. The rest lined the path on their knees, bowing until their foreheads touched the dust.

"They don't even look at us!" said 8 Manik, in amazement.

"They don't dare," said Naked Jaw.

Twin Rabbit ordered the men to halt and walked to the quivering peasant leader. "It is an honor to accept this drink," he said, and quaffed the cup with a swift wave of his arm. "I have come to your house thirsty, and you have given me hospitality. Accept this miserable token of my regard." He pressed something, possibly a jade bead, 8 Manik guessed, into the villager's palm.

The peasant dropped to his knees and touched his forehead to the ground. "My house is yours. My land is yours."

"I must continue this journey," said Twin Rabbit. "But rest assured that I will never forget your hospitality or the warmth of your welcome. Onward."

The band stepped out at its stately pace. Glancing back, 8 Manik saw that the prostrate peasant could not suppress a quick appraising look at his reward to guess at its value. It is amazing, he thought, that not one person noticed the crude imitation of civil behavior made by the men of the band. Twin Rabbit had played his part well enough, but surely any peasant, from however remote a village, would not have mistaken these men for a noble's retinue. This village was on the main route to Palenque. The inhabitants must often have greeted embassies from other city-states. Clearly, they had known all of the accepted phrases. I guess people just don't look at each other, he concluded.

Once over the crest of the hill, Twin Rabbit called a halt and flew into a rage. "I saw you gawking around," he screamed at the men of the front of the band. "What kind of warrior would do that? His eyes must be ahead, on the future, to guard his lord. And you," he said, turning to the boy concubine, "how could you let that peasant place the cup in my hand? Don't you know anything? You should have rushed forward to take the cup and carry it to me!" He delivered a mighty slap to the boy's cheek that nearly knocked him to the ground. "I must never be out of the shade," Twin Rabbit screamed at Naked Jaw. "Wherever I move, you must move with me! That was as sorry a display as I have ever seen in my entire life."

The men who strode over the hilltop so proudly now hung their heads like scolded children. A few stared at their toes as they shifted their feet in the dust.

"Don't look down!" screamed Twin Rabbit, "When corrected, a lord's closest followers must stare straight forward." The chins jerked up as the men hastened to comply.

"This was enough to fool ignorant villagers," concluded Twin Rabbit. "But when we reach a city, we would be immediately unmasked. You must do better, and I know you can. Now let's march on in something approaching decent order."

The march continued on into the sweltering afternoon. Moving on the main route, the band encountered villages nearly every hour, and at each the ceremony of hospitality and obeisance was repeated.   With practice, the men became more imperious and distant in their behavior, and even Twin Rabbit had to admit that the performance was improving. At first the men seemed resentful of his criticism, but as they day wore on they began to assume the prerogatives of dominance with increasing self-assurance.

It was late in the afternoon when the minor city of Chinikiha came into view. To the right a second trail, which led off toward Calakmul, a rising power of southern Yucatan, wound its way up the hill toward them. Coming up the slope was a band of warriors wearing embroidered cloaks and carrying their spears at the ready. To the rear, under a sunshade far larger than that over Twin Rabbit, strode a noble with a proud gait, though the expression on his face was hidden in shadow.

"Stop, men, and look away to the west," ordered Twin Rabbit hastily. "It is not polite to stare at a great lord as he approaches."

8 Manik noticed that the advancing soldiers were also looking away, toward the north, their pace slowing as they came. At the intersection of the paths, they also stopped and so the two bands stood, ostensibly looking away, but surreptitiously catching as much of a view of each other as they could from the corners of their eyes.

A dwarf waddled out on his short legs to hail Twin Rabbit. He began with a low sweeping bow, then began to chant in a weird, keening voice. "It is well to meet one from a far off land and fortunate that the roads we travel on are broad enough for all to travel in comfort." He raised his head from his bow and stood silent as if expecting a reply.

The band froze, no one knowing who should speak or what they should say. For a noble to speak for himself would be demeaning. The dwarf must be a scribe-spokesman, which made him both educated and a curiosity of great value in enlivening the life of a court. Once it had begun, the pause seemed to grow until it enveloped the entire crossroads.

"Talk to him," Twin Rabbit hissed to his bodyguard.

"What should I say?" the flustered man blundered back.

"Accept his gracious greetings and say that we are unworthy of such fine company." Twin Rabbit's face was taut with anger and fear.

The bodyguard stepped forward one hesitant step and made a clumsy imitation of the dwarf's florid bow. "We ...uh... accept your greeting, I mean your gracious greeting. We are unworthy of such fine company as yours," he finally managed to say.

If the dwarf took any notice of the awkwardness of this speech, no change of expression on his bland face gave any indication. Instead, he repeated the bow and continued, "My master, the cahal of the central district of Calakmul, is traveling on this road to celebrate the important anniversary of the reign of his lord's friend and ally, Pakal the Great, leader of Palenque. His business is entirely lawful and peaceful, as I am sure your own is as well."

8 Manik had to admire the gracious flow of language from the little man before him. The role of a scribe required many skills beyond mere reading and writing. Scribes served as advisers, masters of etiquette, and teachers of rhetoric. It was

they who trained the young lords to the requirements of their station. As he listened to the little man, 8 Manik thought he heard the dialect of Tikal in his speech. This would not be strange; for scribes were often hired by leaders in smaller city-states to imitate the manners of great cities.

"Uh, our way is piecemeal," began the bodyguard and one member of the band uttered an involuntary bark of laughter, which he cut short. "I mean our way is peaceful," corrected the humiliated bodyguard. "As well," he added lamely. There was another pause.

Naked Jaw looked across at 8 Manik and rolled his eyes. He seemed to be enjoying the obvious discomfort of Twin Rabbit as he squirmed in the shadow of the sunshade.

Looking exasperated, Twin Rabbit stepped forward and joined the conversation. "I must ask your apology for the crudeness of our speech," he began, addressing the dwarf but clearly intending that the cahal in the other party hear his words. "My scribe was, unfortunately, drowned when crossing the Usamacinta just a few days ago. Being short of time, I was unable to obtain the services of one who has the required training and am forced to use my personal retainer instead."

The dwarf gave Twin Rabbit a calculating look, and bowed yet a third time. "I will convey your situation to my lord," he said. "Extraordinary circumstances may require adjustments in the conduct of polite intercourse." He stepped back to the shade of the cahal's canopy and the two whispered silently for a few minutes.

To 8 Manik's amazement, the lord waddled out toward Twin Rabbit. He was short and enormously fat with an embroidered cloak so thick that 8 Manik did not believe anyone could endure the heat of the afternoon sunshine. Huge jades adorned his ears, and the hematite mirror on his chest was the largest 8 Manik had ever seen. "I am Kan Yax, Cahal of Calakmul and lord of the central district," he announced in a voice that was pleasant and cultured. "I imagine that you and I travel on the same road for the same purpose."

Twin Rabbit was on familiar ground now, and he replied with growing confidence. "I am far from worthy to travel on the road with one from such an eminent center of culture as Calakmul. My own native land of Naj Tunich, while a proud and independent locality, pales beside the growing glory of your center."

"Naj Tunich is a land well known to me and famous for its beauty," replied Kan Yax. "Truly the gods smiled when they created that happy valley."

8 Manik relaxed as he heard the bland and stereotyped compliments falling from Kan Yax's lips. No one who had ever been to Naj Tunich would regard it as beautiful, nor was it located in a valley. The praise was the sort of comment made by someone who knew nothing else to say and wished to observe the elementary rules of propriety.

"And you are sent to salute the Lord Pakal on the completion of this major cycle of days in his rule over Palenque?" asked Twin Rabbit. This question had an edge on it, for it highlighted the fact that Kan Yak had been sent by his kalomte and thus did not hold the status which Twin Rabbit claimed as kalomte of a center. As a ruler of Naj Tunich, a small but sovereign city, Twin Rabbit could claim precedence over Kan Yax, a mere cahal. Still the fact that Calakmul was a dynamic and rising state, which commanded far greater wealth and power than a poor, and remote one complicated the situation, for Kan Yax clearly had a far more impressive entourage than Twin Rabbit.

If Kan Yax took offense at this direct reference to his status as a subordinate, no trace of it appeared on his jowly face. "I go where my lord sends me," he said in a jovial tone. "It is unfortunate that my lord could not come himself, but a sudden illness has overwhelmed him and it is not wise for him to move from one place to another."

Such an excuse, 8 Manik thought, would not go far to assuage Pakal's anger at the absence of the ruler of an important ally at such an important event. If someone were ill, a younger brother or heir might stand in for the ruler, but to send an underling was a calculated snub. Was Pakal waning in influence as he aged? A decade ago, the kalomte of Calakmul would have been carried on his dying litter to attend.

"May the gods ensure his quick return to health," Twin Rabbit answered promptly, but 8 Manik could see his thoughts racing ahead. Trouble between Calakmul and Palenque would tear the whole northern world upside apart, with every center forced to choose between them.

"Perhaps you could aid me," Twin Rabbit added suddenly. "Being so far from my homeland, I am not familiar with the path we are to travel. If your party could lead us, it would be a great assistance in our travels."

A good move, thought 8 Manik. This way he has us at his back instead of being behind us. We grant him precedence of place at our own request and thus do not suffer a loss of prestige at having to trail behind him.

"I will order my men to push ahead," said Kan Yax, "so that no one could mistake you as being part of our procession. It would not do for the kalomte of a sovereign state, such as yourself, to be perceived, however falsely, as following a lowly cahal such as I, even one from so glorious a center as Calakmul."

Worried about an attack from his rear, thought 8 Manik. I guess everyone has to think about the men behind him as well as where he is going.

"We should arrive in Palenque by midday tomorrow," Kan Yax continued. "I'm sure that I will see you at the palace when you go to present your respects to the exalted leader."

Twin Rabbit looked concerned. "I had not planned to arrive so early. It was my intent to make my obeisance in the early hours of the following day."

Kan Yax raised a courtly eyebrow in surprise. "Surely to delay and sleep in the city of a great lord without begging permission is to risk giving great offense," He seemed to be prompting Twin Rabbit to recant and avoid the diplomatic misstep.

"In the south our customs are different," said Twin Rabbit. "We prefer to approach the great after our morning bath as a symbol of deference and not to give offense."

"As you wish," said Kan Yax. "I only hope that the great Pakal is aware of the etiquette of your region. I would not wish to be the one who offended a man of such power. What if he decided to make me captive and forced me to play in the sacred ball game? I'm so fat, my opponent might mistake me for the ball!" He tittered at his own attempt at humor.

"I follow the ways of my city whatever the consequences," said Twin Rabbit, imperiously.

"Let us hope the consequences will not be too severe," answered Kan Yax, and shouted for his men to advance. They moved off in fair order while Twin Rabbit kept his own party in check. Once they were out of earshot, Kan Yax must have sent some other order forward, for the party quickened its pace. Clearly, 8 Manik thought, the cahal didn't want to be associated in any way with the party on the road behind him.

"Forward at half pace!" shouted Twin Rabbit. The men started off slowly, and with each step seemed to move with even less enthusiasm.

I wonder what has slowed their pace, 8 Manik asked himself. Maybe it was the resplendent of Yax Kan and the elegant robes of his followers. When the men came from the forest to the path, they had been dressed more wonderfully than they ever had in their entire lives. They were thrilled by the luxury of their new station. Marching in formation they had seemed unstoppable. Now they felt like a band of overdressed nothings, outshone by the attendants of an underling of a second-class center.

Naked Jaw tapped 8 Manik on the shoulder to get his attention. With a flick of his head he drew attention to the scowl on Twin Rabbit's face. The noble glared from one side of the path to another, eager to find fault with his followers.

"There's a village over the next hill," he shouted. "When you approach it, I don't want a single eye to waver. People judge nobility by the way a man moves. He must conduct himself with assurance and reserve. If any one of you slouches or looks around like some oafish peasant, I'll have his fingernails torn off as soon as we leave town!"

The men kept their order, but their confidence was still shaken. At the crest of the hill, they found themselves looking down on a hamlet much like the others they had passed that day. Those who had gathered to gape at the cahal of Calakmul were just beginning to disperse, and the headman turned back toward the road to continue his duties of obeisance.

"Straight ahead!" hissed Twin Rabbit. "No wandering eyes."

8 Manik struggled to keep his gaze forward, but the urge to glance aside was irresistible. The headman came forward with a knot of villagers to offer a drink. As Twin Rabbit reached to receive the cup from the boy concubine, 8 Manik, knowing that the noble's attention must be elsewhere, flicked his eyes across the crowd. A face jumped out from the rest. It was his son, Muan, standing also transfixed, his mouth opening in an involuntary cry of recognition.

CHAPTER TEN

With no time to stop Muan from crying out, 8 Manik shot his foot out and caught Twin Rabbit's ankle as he stepped forward to receive the proffered cup.

"Father," shouted Muan, his words ringing out across the crowd, but even as he spoke, Twin Rabbit lurched off the boy concubine's shoulder and fell against the headman of the village. The crowd of onlookers gasped in horror and amazement that turned to screams of fear as Naked Jaw whipped an obsidian knife from his breechcloth and leaped forward. He crouched over Twin Rabbit's prostrate body, every muscle alert and ready for an attack, holding the crowd a bay. They shrank back in horror. Carried down by the force of Twin Rabbit's fall, the headman writhed on the ground, screaming in terror.

"I didn't do it! I didn't do it," screamed the headman.

"Form a circle with your spears at the ready!" shouted Naked Jaw.

"Betrayal!" bellowed Twin Rabbit. "Someone will pay for this!"

The spectators did not wait to hear more. They turned and fled for the fields as if expecting the men of the procession to charge after them. Within a minute, the open space before the cluster of huts was empty of its inhabitants and the rapidly forming circle of bandits looked out at a deserted village with Muan alone remaining, stunned by the confusion.

Twin Rabbit scrambled to his feet, seized a spear from one of the bandits, and began beating the headman who huddled at his feet. "You idiot!" the noble screamed, "How dare you touch a man of my rank?"

"But great ahau," began the headman. "I did nothing. I was just. I just handed your libation to your." Each phrase was punctuated by the thud of blows falling across his back as he groveled in the dust.

8 Manik stared intently at Muan, desperately willing him to keep silent. He pointed toward the shadow of a hut near the edge of the clearing. Muan stood as if transfixed, and then he reluctantly began making his way in the direction 8 Manik indicated. Trying to look as unobtrusive as possible, 8 Manik sidled off to join him. As soon as they were sheltered from the others, 8 Manik threw his arms around Muan's shoulders. To his amazement, he found tears rolling down his cheeks and was unable to speak as the emotion of the moment choked him.

In the end it was Muan who was able to speak first. "Father, you're alive. We thought they would have killed you by now."

"I'm in no danger," said 8 Manik. "Have you found Hunapu?"

"No one knows where Hunapu is. I was delayed on my trip south and Ix found me within a day. When we returned and found the burned compound, we feared at first that Hunapu had died in the fire. Then a neighbor woman said that she had seen the woman and two boys leave the compound just after the fire broke out. From her description, one of them had to be Hunapu. We asked and asked, but her way had been lost in all the excitement. After searching for days, I decided to come to Palenque to find this madman and force him to tell me where Hunapu is."

"How can you force a man surrounded by forty armed henchmen to tell you anything?" asked 8 Manik.

"I had no way of knowing he had so many men with them," Muan flared. "Everyone told me he left with only three. In any case, it didn't matter. If I found him with one or a hundred, I would kill him."

8 Manik was stunned to hear Muan talk this way. He'd never heard such determination in his voice before, never before seen hatred glaring in his eyes. He's grown, he thought, he's become a man. I would try to kill Twin Rabbit too. But now it is my job to keep Muan alive. He hasn't a chance against those men.

"We'll do it together," he said, hoping to defuse his son's anger. "But first we must think of Hunapu. If you rush in and kill this man, there's no chance the boy will survive."

"But we can't just stand here and do nothing," blurted Muan. "Maybe if Twin Rabbit is dead, his servants will listen to us. We could buy Hunapu's freedom."

"And if they don't listen to us?" said 8 Manik. "If they decide to murder your wife and mother in revenge? What will you do then? These men are talented at killing. We must wait them out."

"Wait!" Muan's voice was full of loathing.

"Yes!" said 8 Manik, feeling his impatience rising in his voice. "I have been working on the bodyguards. They are brave men, but foolish. If I keep talking, I think I may be able to get them to reveal where Hunapu is. Then I can get the information to you and you can go back and rescue him while I play along with them."

A moment of doubt flickered over Muan's face. "But if this noble gets to Palenque, how could we kill him there?"

"I've been to Palenque a hundred times," said 8 Manik. "A city is the easiest place to lose a pursuer or to stalk someone. I know vendors in the market who can help us." One lie was piling on top of another. What would Muan think of him when he found them out? No time to worry about that now. "For now, we must play for time," 8 Manik concluded, his words lame in his ears as he said them.

A desperate scream for mercy bellowed out across the village. How much of a beating could the poor man take?

"I've got to go back before I'm missed," whispered 8 Manik. "Follow us at a distance. When everyone is asleep tonight, I'll slip away and we can plan together."

Muan nodded his assent. 8 Manik grabbed the young man's hand and put it on his own head as a blessing. He didn't know why he did it. It should be the old man who blesses the younger, but somehow the gesture seemed to comfort them both.

"Tonight," repeated 8 Manik, and slipped back to the group. The unconscious body of the headman lay in the dust, rivulets of blood flowing from his back and arms. The two bodyguards stood above him, leaning on their spears as if they were a couple of agricultural workers who had just completed a hard day's work in the fields. Twin Rabbit was prancing about the empty village, shaking with the emotion of the moment.

"I am the Lord of Tikal," he screamed to no one in particular. "I'm the greatest ruler in the land! Master of all I survey! I am the favored of the gods. None may touch me save those to whom I have granted royal permission!" Flecks of spit flew from his lips in great arching curves as he bellowed into the vacant village. "The people of the world bow down before me!"

8 Manik slipped into the knot of anxious-looking men who were staring in dumb amazement. Gradually and without trying to draw attention to himself, he wriggled his way to a position next to Naked Jaw.

"He's possessed," muttered one of the men.

"He's leading us to our doom," said another, voicing what many others must be thinking.

"Silence!" hissed Naked Jaw. "There will be no talk like that around here."

"But look at him," muttered one of the veterans of the band. "If he acts like that in Palenque, we'll be slaughtered. I've seen the glances you give him. You know that he is crazy as much as we do."

Naked Jaw turned a glare on him that would have smashed rocks to powder. When he spoke, however, his words trickled out in a whisper of pure menace. "You will be quiet, or I will find a way to make you quiet."

The man who had spoken blanched.

"Do you want to join that man on the ground and be beaten senseless?" asked Naked Jaw. "This is no time for disunity. We are in the open. I have no idea who is watching us, but I know that everything we do will be reported in Palenque before we arrive."

"This is madness," the man muttered, almost under his breath.

"The gods alone can say who is mad and who isn't," said Naked Jaw. "I am marching on, and if you do not march with us, we cannot permit you to escape and tell your tale. You will come with us and you will keep your mouth shut, or you will never speak again."

The man relapsed into sullen silence. The surrounding men rolled their eyes in disbelief, but no one said a word.

Twin Rabbit's fit ended as suddenly as it had begun. There was a long moment of silence as he turned to confront the men who were staring at him. The time seemed to stretch endlessly as each side groped for something to say. The longer it went on, the more intense the silence became. "Well, then," said Twin Rabbit as if nothing had happened. "We must push on. We will not be staying in Chinikha. We will make our best speed until we reach Palenque."

8 Manik thought that he might hear grumbling about another forced march, but the situation was so tense that no one wanted to be held responsible for making trouble. The line reformed its old pattern and the order was given to move along. The men stepped out in surprisingly good order. Behind them in the village, the headman groaned and stirred in the dust of the plaza.

8 Manik permitted himself one furtive glance over his shoulder, to see if he could catch one quick glimpse of Muan following along the trail. He saw nothing, which was as it should be. If Naked Jaw or Twin Rabbit saw Muan, 8 Manik was sure they would send one of the bandits back to set a trap to eliminate him. Like his brother Ix, Muan

was an excellent tracker who loved to creep up on game. It made no sense to look back, since it would only increase the chance that Muan would be discovered, but the urge to look, to know what Muan was doing and where he was, was irresistible.

It did not take long for the tropical dusk to close into nightfall, and the men quickened their pace as soon as they knew they could not be seen. On either side of the broad path, the forest loomed up in pitch darkness. The cries of night birds joined the chorus of insects. The stars glittered down through the swath cut in the forest canopy when the path ran beside peasant fields on broad streams. The red planet seemed to hang at the end of the trail, calling them onward. Three more hours passed before Twin Rabbit called a halt. A few men flopped to the ground in exhaustion, but he cursed them for soiling their finery. Those who had been less impulsive removed their clothing and folded it before dropping down to the ground to rest.

Naked Jaw leaned over and whispered in Twin Rabbit's each with a voice full of reason and menace. "If you push the men too hard, they will desert you."

In the gloom, 8 Manik could see Twin Rabbit's proud profile as he turned to answer. "I am leading these men on the paths that fate has laid out for them. If they follow me, fortunes so great they cannot imagine them will be theirs. The gods have selected me as their leader and protector."

"That may be quite true," said Naked Jaw, "but the men are exhausted. You have been driving them all day. Even the best of men will crumple to the earth if they do not get adequate rest."

"It is not my choice but that of the gods which sends us on this pace," replied Twin Rabbit. "The heavens themselves have prepared the signs for our success. I do not know if your men can accomplish it, but I know I must be in Palenque tomorrow night. I know where Pakal will be tomorrow night, and I know he will be alone."

This comment astounded 8 Manik. The great lords were never alone. They moved in a circle of courtiers and guards, protecting them, attending them. Musicians played when a great lord such as Pakal approached. Scribes had to be there to record the decisions he made. Young men, eager for advancement, were always on duty, prepared to flatter and fawn at the slightest opportunity.

"Tomorrow is the night," repeated Twin Rabbit. "Tell the men to get up. There is not a moment to lose."

His bodyguards obediently lurched to their feet and started passing the word that it was time to start. A few men grumbled but were quickly hushed by their comrades. After witnessing the brutal beating administered in the plaza, 8 Manik thought, there was little inclination to revolt.

On through the night the men staggered, their travel broken by only the briefest periods of rest. Although they were moving closer to Palenque, the alternative passage of forest and field in the darkness became a repetitive nightmare. It seemed that they were hardly moving at all, that their journey was endless and unmarked, with no progress at all.

It was during one of the brief periods of rest that the sun finally showed itself above the eastern horizon. Once 8 Manik was able to orient himself, he realized that they would probably arrive in

Palenque just before dusk. To this extent, Twin Rabbit's plan seemed to be working just as he anticipated.

Unlike many Mayan cities, Palenque stood on the higher edge of a broad and undulating plain, so that it commanded a wide view over the fields to the south. Some said that Pakal's ancestors had placed it there for defense against their neighboring city-states, so that no army could surprise them. Some said it was located over great and miraculous caves that led the way to an underworld chamber where the ruling family could tap the powers of the dark lords below. Certainly, Palenque was not one of the great trading centers. Though vendors came to sell to its populace, most of the trade of the Usamacinta valley ran well to the east. A small, proud, independent locality with an exaggerated sense of its own importance, it had long been either derided or ignored by larger Mayan centers. In the last one hundred years, however, Palenque had enjoyed enormous success in the field of battle so that it now commanded tribute from a broad swath of cities and villages, which had once been independent. Under Pakal, it had grown to rival the much larger cities of the Mayan world, and the glory of its architecture was considered a marvel.

As 8 Manik looked across the plateau toward Palenque, the bright red temples glowed in the light of the morning sun, as if somehow blood had flowed up from the earth unstaunched. 8 Manik had traveled to Palenque before and every time he had looked at it, it had seemed alive with promise. The city was vibrant and its people spent their wealth with a careless profligacy that was good news for any trader. To say of another trader that he bargained like a man from Palenque was no compliment, for it meant he was careless of small details while being grasping and domineering of others. Now the menace of Palenque reached out toward them. It was so dynamic that any attempt on it seemed insane.

Something stirred and 8 Manik looked over to find Naked Jaw standing by his side. The bandit leader didn't speak at first. He gazed at the city in the distance. 8 Manik wondered if the bandit leader shared his sense of foreboding.

"We're being followed," said Naked Jaw. "He's a good tracker and I couldn't catch any trace of him until dawn. It will be harder to escape detection during the daytime."

"Why are you telling me this?" asked 8 Manik, struggling to keep the anxiety out of his voice. He longed to rush back and warn Muan, but that would simply give him away.

"I thought you might be able to tell me who he was. I saw you slip off back in the village, while our mutual friend was bludgeoning the headman."

"I had to relieve myself. Would you prefer I pissed all over the poor fellow while he was being abused?"

"You suddenly seem very demure," muttered Naked Jaw. "I didn't notice you being so delicate on prior stops"

"We never stopped to so long in a village before," explained 8 Manik. "One doesn't behave the same way there that one does in the forest. As a matter of fact, I did run into a young man there. He was peeking through the chinks in the wall of a house at what was going on. Maybe he became curious and decided to follow us."

A nagging voice in 8 Manik's mind told him he was explaining too much. He could have kicked himself. As a trader, he'd learned not only to listen to the words a man spoke, but also to how long he kept talking. The more a man spoke, the less likely what he said was true. Now he could hear himself rattling on, inserting irrelevant and plausible details, his story sounding more false with every word.

"Perhaps," said Naked Jaw. "Maybe I don't need to send someone back to ambush him."

A trap, thought 8 Manik. If I agree, he'll know I have someone to protect. If I tell him to send someone, I could be arranging for the doom of my own child. He shrugged, "That's not my affair," he said, willing his voice to sound bored and indifferent.

Naked Jaw strolled away without further comment. 8 Manik squatted down and lowered his head, trying to look as if he were too exhausted to care about anything. He put a hand to his forehead so that he could sneak a sideways glance and track what Naked Jaw was doing. The leader was standing with a group of men, talking easily. He didn't seem to be giving orders, but 8 Manik knew that Naked Jaw would not send someone away openly. Muan, who must have stopped when the band made its halt, would be watching to see if anyone were sent in his direction. Naked Jaw would probably suggest that his hunter simply lag slowly to the rear, then wait motionless beside the path to waylay Muan. The knot of men broke up with a burst of laughter.

"Gather round," Twin Rabbit ordered, startling the tired group to life. The men hoisted themselves to their feet and shuffled toward him, their eyes glazed with fatigue, their shoulders slumped with exhaustion. "Gather round," Twin Rabbit repeated, raising his voice as if trying to force more energy into their slack bodies. "Look over there, men. There in the sunlight on that far hill you see the red pyramids of Palenque, the greatest city of the north. That is the city where I was raised, in the great palace that stands below the temple that Pakal has finished. Palenque is a magnificent city, but I tell you today. That city is yours! I grant you that city under the leadership of Naked Jaw who will become its kalomte!"

The men of the band looked at each other in amazement. They were ready, 8 Manik thought, for a quick and miraculously successful raid, a bit of snatch and grab followed by a thrilling retreat with their booty. The idea that they might become lords must sound bizarre.

"I know this sounds amazing to you, " Twin Rabbit continued. "I know that you believe there is no way such things could come to pass. But I swear to you this night, you yourselves will see that the power of Ix Chel, the goddess of the moon, will devour the Mars beast. This red star, the one that the great Lord Pakal has worshipped above all others since his youth, will be eclipsed by the moon, my patroness. The days of Pakal's reign are over. Our day has come. It is written on the heavens above us."

Twin Rabbit stopped and looked about him, waiting for the men to burst into cheers. They stood in glum silence. 8 Manik wondered if they had heard, or understood, a single word.

"On, men!" Twin Rabbit shouted. The men turned and started up the path, stumbling along like an army of the dead. 8 Manik and Naked Jaw fell into position behind Twin Rabbit. "Idiots," they heard him mutter to himself. "I lead an army of idiots."

The pace they set was slower than any he had seen so far. The group inched its way up the next rise and over the top. There was plenty of time for 8 Manik to stoop to adjust the straps of his sandals. From his knee he shot an appraising glance across the group, trying to spot the members that Naked Jaw had joked with just minutes before. As far as he could tell, all were present. Maybe Naked Jaw hadn't told one to leave the group and ambush Muan. A hurried set of steps brought him back into his place in line.

"This has been a strange journey," said Naked Jaw in a low voice. "A time of marvels, messages from the gods, sudden death and lingering life. But in all that time, do you know what puzzles me the most?"

"What?" asked 8 Manik, wondering why the bandit leader had suddenly become talkative.

"The strange business of that missing tapir at the cave," said Naked Jaw.

"The tapir?"

"Yes, the one that seemed to come back to life and move up the path and then die again not two hundred paces from the entrance. How do you explain that?"

"Perhaps one of your men wanted to steal it and keep it for himself," said 8 Manik. "They are bandits and there's never so much meat to eat that a man doesn't want more."

"The men knew we were leaving the next day," said Naked Jaw. "A thief might have eaten what he could then, but to do so would have meant lighting a fire and being discovered. The body of the tapir was left untouched. My men may be thieves, market vendor, but they never steal without a reason."

"One of the bodyguards, perhaps?" said 8 Manik. He didn't like the trend of this conversation.

"They were with Twin Rabbit in the depths of the cave. Taking the tapir outside would only mean that they would have less to eat on the journey."

"A great mystery," said 8 Manik.

"Not so great a mystery. The only reason to steal the food and throw it away would be an attempt to delay the journey. The only person with any motive to disrupt the journey was you."

"You didn't come to this conclusion just now," said 8 Manik. "You must have reasoned this out soon after the tapir was discovered. Why didn't you present your theory before? Whether you were right or wrong, Twin Rabbit would have seized on the chance to dispose of me."

"Let's say that I didn't want you eliminated," said Naked Jaw. "I just want you to remember that you owe your life to me."

Some dark, contrary impulse stirred in 8 Manik's soul. "You should hope that I never repay you what I owe you," he hissed. "I owe to you the kidnapping of my grandson, my captivity on this insane journey which will get us all killed, days of brutal hiking, witnessing the deaths of innocent men at the whim of this lunatic, my son's life in peril, and the seduction of that girl. I owe you a great deal, you master of death. Do you want me to thank you for my life? Do you want me to kiss your feet? Don't dream of the gratitude I will offer you."

Naked Jaw laughed and clapped 8 Manik on the shoulder. "I wondered who it was who was following us. It must be your son. Thanks for letting me know, old vendor. Maybe I should have been a trader instead of an outlaw. Outwitting you is a great deal less dangerous than stealing."

8 Manik cursed himself for his stupidity. How did he let that reference to Muan get into his conversation? He saw now that Naked Jaw had been needling him all along until he would lose control and reveal what he knew.

The urge to get even with Naked Jaw swept over him. He wanted to lash back, to invent some brilliant story that would explain the inclusion of his son in his list of complaints. He could say that he thought Muan was in danger searching for little Hunapu in Tikal where the baby was hidden. He could say that he had pretended the pursuer was his son in order to fool Naked Jaw. Even as he rehearsed these lines in his brain, he knew they were futile. To attempt them would simple confirm to Naked Jaw that his suspicions were correct.

One of the hardest lessons a vendor had to learn was the way to react when some one had bested him. 8 Manik had seen young sellers return time after time to those who had cheated them, desperate for revenge. Each time they told themselves that they were turning the tables. They knew how this man had cheated them and he would never do it again. Better still, they would swindle him and get back the profit they had lost. So they would patronize the men who had bested them, only to be taken again.

The best way to deal with a crook was to leave him alone. Take the loss and learn from it. There were plenty of honest vendors in the markets and he would be honest with them. Over the years, he saw those devious vendors working harder and harder to cheat the few who were simple enough to keep coming back, all the while missing the business of those who had learned to avoid them. If the gods had created a just universe, this was their justice. To expect victory was simply to invite repeated defeat.

Naked Jaw looked at his quiet face, then clapped him on the shoulder again. "Don't worry, old man, your secret is safe with me. And your son will be too, as long as you don't cause me any trouble."

"Naked Jaw," called Twin Rabbit, "come over here. I need to talk to you for a minute."

As he watched Naked Jaw in conference, panic swelled through 8 Manik. He was certain now that Naked Jaw would have one of his men slip to the side of the path to waylay Muan as he followed. It would be simplicity itself. The man would simply wait until the path crossed another crest and the step into some underbrush. There would be no way that Muan would notice the absence of a single figure and no time to react even if he did. Like the fowler, his life would be over in a single devastating attack with no chance for self defense..

8 Manik sat down at the end of the path. He had to find a way to warn Muan of the danger. Picking up a stick as if he were doodling in the dust, he made two lines parallel with three dots above the top line. Muan could easily read the number as 13 in the bar and dot numeration of the Maya, with each bar being a unit of 5 and each dot a one. Lazily 8 Manik traced a circle around the number to indicate that they were a group. Further up the path, he inscribed two bars and two dots in a circle with one dot off to the side to indicate the hunter. A leaf dropped between the hunter and the group might suggest an ambush. It seemed unlikely that Muan

would see it and recognize it, but 8 Manik could think of no other way to communicate without giving away Muan's presence to everyone in the party.

"I need two men here to carry my consort," shouted Twin Rabbit. "She is too fatigued to travel on her own, and no great lord would ever allow his wife to be so fatigued."

The men were too exhausted to grumble. A pair gave up the poles of their spears to serve as side rails of an improvised stretcher. The bed of the litter was made of cloth strips wound between the polls. The young girl lay down on the contraption and was hoisted as if she were a wounded soldier carried home from battle.

As the men in theprocession lurched to their feet, 8 Manik saw Naked Jaw talking with one of the men. He was burly and his eyes were set close together. As the procession began to get under way, this man idled out of position, falling toward the rear. For a second, 8 Manik thought of rushing at him, doing anything to destroy the progress of the procession. He wanted to scream out to Muan to turn and run. It would be useless. If Muan were keeping a safe distance, he wouldn't hear the warning. 8 Manik would have to trust to his son to avoid trouble. Muan is a bright boy, he thought without a great deal of conviction.

There was no need for Twin Rabbit to urge the men to walk slowly now. Many of them were staggering with fatigue. The lines were ragged as they plodded stolidly onward. The pyramids of Palenque seemed to creep toward them, gradually growing more distinct against the green hills behind them. The road was almost deserted and the villages deserted of all but the very old or very young. The whole world, it seemed, had preceded them to the great city to celebrate at the command of Lord Pakal.

As they approached the city, the clusters of houses appeared more frequently in the fields. An occasional toddler might wander from the courtyards in curiosity, only to be snatched back by an imperious, maternal arm. Finally they came to a compound much larger than the rest, five thatch-roofed houses surrounding a central plaza, sealed off from the outside by a wall of stakes. Twin Rabbit directed the men to enter, and they filed in.

The rooms were deserted; the hearths, cold. Still, everything was in spotless order. Fine textiles hung from the rafters and elaborately patterned mats covered all the floors. The walls were lined with chests. One of the men opened the lid and found it stuffed with even more elaborate textiles. It looked as if the compound had been abandoned only a day before. The men wandered around, looking about with blank, exhausted stares. The litter bearers had lowered their load, and the girl stood up to join the group.

"My dear," said Twin Rabbit, "since you are the only woman here, you must undertake the task of hospitality. In the cookhouse you will find ample food, I am sure. The rest must remain silent. Were our presence discovered, it might wreck my plans."

"What place is this?" 8 Manik whispered to Naked Jaw. He felt strange asking questions as if they were close friends, but their shared distaste for Twin Rabbit gave them something in common.

"I have no idea," Naked Jaw replied in a low voice, but Twin Rabbit overheard him and snapped around, a triumphant gleam in his eyes.

"Allow me to welcome you," he said with formality, "to the country residence of Chan Bahlum, current heir to the throne of Palenque."

CHAPTER ELEVEN

The effect of this statement on the listening men was overwhelming. Chan Bahlum was famous, not only as Pakal's oldest son, but for the fact that he had six toes, which was regarded as marvelous and a sign of his exceptional nature. As heir to the throne, he had led the armies of Palenque in battle for nearly two decades once Pakal became too old to take to the field of battle in person. Of course he and his entire household would be at the ceremonies. There had been no need to post a guard, since no one would dare to offend so powerful a figure.

After their initial shock, the men immediately began pilfering the contents of the rooms. One found an elaborately carved jade figurine on the floor beside one of the storage boxes. He carried it out to the sunlit patio, turning it over and over in his hand.

"What kind of man can leave a jade like this lying on the floor?" he marveled. "This is worth more than all my father's house and lands put together!"

"Look what I found here," cried another, throwing open a chest and pulling out elaborately woven garments. "Quick, let's divide these things up!"

A half dozen men clustered round him, tugging at the valuables, claiming them for their own. Two of them grabbed a woman's cape at the same time and began pulling on opposite ends.

"Mine!" shouted one.

"I had it first," yelled the other.

"Quiet!" roared Naked Jaw, clouting the nearer on the back of the head with a great swipe of his open palm. The men fell silent. "This is not a raid on some peasant hut. If we succeed, each of you will be dividing more than a hundred times the goods in that chest. You will be quiet or I will quiet you permanently."

The men fell silent, daunted by his rage.

"Here comes the girl with the food," said 8 Manik, in the vague hope that he could start another hubbub. Given the deserted fields they had passed, he had little hope that the men in the compound would be discovered, but it seemed that any interruption in Twin Rabbit's plan could only be of benefit. The girl had returned with a huge platter of tortillas and a great bowl of cold, cooked black beans. The men rushed to her, suddenly aware of how hungry they were. 8 Manik's hopes for a quarrel were dashed, for the men became quiet as they used the tortillas to scoop up the beans and stuff them in their mouths. They ate so quickly that they couldn't have made noise if they wanted to. The only sound was the slurping of the famished men, Twin Rabbit joined Naked Jaw and 8 Manik.

"You are wise not to eat," he said. "In an hour, all these men will be asleep. A man who is hungry is more alert. We must prepare for the journey we take tonight, for the three of us go alone. I will arrange to have my men follow us just before dawn. They will travel the more swiftly because I have denied them food as well."

As he spoke, the last slanting rays of the sun left the roofs of the compound and the patio darkened. 8 Manik looked to the deepening blue of the sky to search out the brilliant planet that never travels far from the sun. This planet was the brother of the sun, one of the hero twins who had brought light and life to the earth. The doorways of many temples throughout the Mayan world were lined up so that the rays of this planet would shine in in on the day of its reappearance as the morning or evening star.

Only an ignorant peasant child did not realize that the morning and evening star were one and the same thing. As the morning star, it cleared the road of the sun across the sky. As the evening star, it trailed the sun, guarding him from an attack from the rear. In the highlands of Mexico, it was believed that the two were rivals and battled during the day within the dark halls of the underworld. For the Maya, the two were protectors of the world order. In the great observatories, the priests who were charged with predicting the reappearance stood watch every night. Of all the planets, its motions were the most regular and comforting. Tonight it was nowhere to be seen, lost in its passage between the morning and evening sky.

Twin Rabbit must have seen 8 Manik looking up, for he spoke softly. "Are you looking for help from above, merchant? At moonrise tonight, the red planet, the beast that is the special patron of the Lord Pakal, will be pursued, taken by the moon. Tonight, Pakal's star will be eaten, and he along with it.

"The stars…the gods are not mortal," answered 8 Manik.

Twin Rabbit only nodded smugly. "Wait and see. There are things you do not, cannot, know. Those of us who are foresighted have knowledge of our fate. Enjoy the sunset tonight. It will be the last you will observe on the surface of the world. We aren't in the jungle where Naked Jaw could protect you. You will be in the sacred precinct which is my legitimate realm."

"I would never challenge the authority of a lord," replied 8 Manik in a sullen tone.

8 Manik felt all hope slipping away. Exhausted, in despair, he was certain that the man that Naked Jaw had sent off had ambushed Muan. Hunapu was, no doubt, dead as well. Why should they keep him alive? His kidnapping had merely been a ruse to keep his foolish grandfather under control. All of 8 Manik's efforts had failed to protect either his son or his grandson. Soon he would die as well.

He realized that he was exhausted, weaving on his feet. Fatigue was the twin of despair. Ignoring the food that was being wolfed down by the men, he sagged to the plastered floor of the patio, his back leaning against a post. His chin drifted downward and he gave way to the blissful mindlessness of sleep.

At first his sleep was deep and intense, as if he had plunged straight from consciousness into a dark underworld, a land without time. Then, in the darkness, a spot of light came and grew. Standing in the circle of light was a figure with an enormous headdress. With a shudder, 8 Manik realized that it was the North Star, the Black Scorpion, arrayed as he had been in the vision in the cave.

"Why do you doubt me?" asked the god.

"Doubt you?" echoed 8 Manik. He knew the gods could examine men's souls.

"You fear," said the god, "You despair."

"Yes," said 8 Manik. "I fear for the lives of those I love. My son, my grandson, my wife, my other children. What will become of them if I am not able to protect them? I have failed and now some are dead, and all may die."

"All must die in their own time," said the god, "but the time has only arrived for one tonight in the sacred precinct of Palenque."

"Who? Who must die?" gasped 8 Manik.

"The gods never say," said the Black Scorpion, "but do not doubt. All will return from whence it came."

The vision ended as abruptly as it had begun. 8 Manik sank back into the profound depths that only the exhausted can achieve. A black, seemingly endless, withdrawal from the world, which no sound can disturb or change of light can alter, and which leaves no record of the passing hours.

When Naked Jaw shook him awake, 8 Manik staggered back into consciousness. Stiff, confused, he was aware only of a ravenous hunger. He groaned incoherently, making Naked Jaw utter a short, barking laugh.

"You're a tough one to rouse," he said.

"Hungry," said 8 Manik, feeling stupid from the intensity of the sleep.

"Grab some cold tortillas from the cooking hut and get ready in a hurry," said Naked Jaw.

8 Manik rubbed his eyes and struggled to make out the bodies of the sleeping men in the darkness. In the pale gloom of starlight, he felt his way along to the doorway of the cooking house, then explored his way like a blind man until his fingers felt the familiar, leathery touch of a stack of tortillas. He stuffed several in his mouth and immediately regretted his greed, for they were dry and tough and almost impossible to swallow. Finding a drink would be impossible, so he ground

his jaws together in the darkness until a little saliva made it possible to force the food down his throat.

Back in the patio, he sensed the movement of two men near the gateway and felt his way to them. As he approached, he saw that the man talking to Naked Jaw was Twin Rabbit. He held a spear in his right hand and the pouch with the ceremonial flint knife hung from his neck. 8 Manik felt naked, having given up his obsidian blade. Naked Jaw, he was sure, would never go anywhere without some kind of weapon.

"Three of us," said Twin Rabbit. "One for each of the stones which formed the first hearth at the making of the world. The stars you see high overhead in winter, close in line. Pakal and Chan Bahlum say they are going to erect three more great pyramids to honor the founding of the universe."

8 Manik coughed politely to let them know he had joined them. Twin Rabbit turned on him. "What has taken you so long?"

The dry tortillas had thickened 8 Manik's tongue, but in any case Twin Rabbit, not waiting for a reply, turned and disappeared into the darkness. 8 Manik might have lost him in the gloom, but Naked Jaw's quick departure in the same direction let him know which way to travel.

Even though there were only stars to light the way, their progress was rapid. Twin Rabbit was on his home ground, and he twisted through the city with absolute confidence. Gradually, but steadily, the path was rising, as they made their way through the densely settled maze of compounds. Occasionally the red gleam of embers fading on a hearth within a compound showed the way. 8 Manik knew they must be approaching the great plaza that was the center of the sacred precinct.

8 Manik wondered how much of the night had passed. To judge from the way that the fires had burned low, several hours must have elapsed since sunset. He guessed it must be near the middle of the night. Suddenly he bumped into Naked Jaw, who had stopped without a word. The bandit leader whirled and whipped out an obsidian blade. 8 Manik could not withhold a grunt of fright.

"Watch where you're going. I almost killed you," snapped Naked Jaw. "I thought you were someone attacking me from the rear."

"Why did you stop?" asked 8 Manik, but even as he spoke he realized that they were at the main plaza. Before they had been following Twin Rabbit down winding pathways, but now space opened before them and 8 Manik suddenly felt exposed on all sides. In the east, the sky was bright, and, as they paused for a moment, the half moon slid above the horizon, filling the plaza with light. Twin Rabbit had not paused for a second and now stood directly in the center of the open space.

"Look," Twin Rabbit shouted, pointing to the moon.

Following his gesture, 8 Manik saw that the red planet was rising immediately above the moon so that it seemed that the two must touch. The red animal god and the moon goddess were about to become as one. A shudder ran down 8 Manik's spine. Such a grand encounter must presage some event of enormous importance.

"Quickly," shouted Twin Rabbit, all efforts at secrecy cast away, "we must be at the top of the temple at the moment of union!" He raced across the smooth plaster surface to the wide steps that led to the temple beyond. Without thinking, Naked Jaw and 8 Manik rushed after him. The noble reached the stairs and began to climb, cutting a diagonal path across the front of the temple as he ascended. Arriving at the bottom of the stairs, 8 Manik found himself confronting a façade so steep it almost seemed like a cliff. The riser of each step was nearly a foot high and the treads were so narrow that less than half of his foot would fit. Awkwardly, Naked Jaw and 8 Manik followed Twin Rabbit's path, but the distance between them grew ever greater. They were less than half way up when they could see him standing exultantly standing on the level platform in front of the door of the temple building at the summit.

"The red planet is dead," Twin Rabbit shouted to the echoing plaza. He held his lance aloft, shaking it at the sky as if he were challenging all the gods to mortal combat.

8 Manik glanced over his shoulder and saw that Twin Rabbit spoke the truth. The red planet had indeed been eaten by Ix Chel in the constellation of the frog with the three stars of creation nearby. It was at moments such as these that the entire universe went into a state of acute danger, and lords of great cities abandoned their quest for glory and huddled close to the seats of power. The cycles of time, which common men could never understand but which the astronomer priests studied constantly, were moving toward completion.

Scrabbling finally to the top of the pyramid, 8 Manik and Naked Jaw found themselves alone on the platform. The sheer effrontery of their actions dazzled 8 Manik. These were the holiest spaces in the city, where none but noble lords and their priests dared go. Commoners belonged in the plaza, looking up in adoration at their superiors communing with the gods. No commoner in Tikal would dare to climb a temple once it was consecrated. To do so would bring punishment on earth and divine retribution in the afterworld.

Where was Twin Rabbit? Timidly 8 Manik peered into the room of the temple. A single torch flared on the wall, tended, no doubt, by some apprentice priest who came in the middle of the night to light the sanctuary of the god. Everything was still.

"Come here," whispered Naked Jaw. 8 Manik looked around, saw no one, and started back to the doorway.

"Here," came the voice again. Naked Jaw was standing in the shadows. There, at his feet, lay an opening in the floor. "It's a stairway," he said. "He must have gone down."

"Should we go down?" asked 8 Manik.

"It's the only place he could have gone," said Naked Jaw. Only the first steps were visible in the light. After that the darkness was complete. Once on the stairway, however, 8 Manik found the descent was not as hard as he thought. The steps were even, and the walls that closed in on both sides made it easy to keep his balance. He counted the steps as he went down. It seemed as if the numbers were a cord unrolling behind him, a connection to the outside world.

Forty-five steps down in the darkness, Naked Jaw came to a stop. "No more steps." he said, "There must be a corridor. He reached out and recoiled back from the wall before him. "Nothing there: the way is blocked."

"That doesn't make any sense," said 8 Manik. "Who would build a stairway going nowhere?"

"We don't know the sacred ways of priests," said Naked Jaw. 8 Manik could almost see him shrug in the darkness. Not a star to be seen, he thought.

"Not a star in the sky," the words of the old man came back to him. "Going downward, doubling back."

"Down to a light," muttered 8 Manik. "The staircase must cross back against itself."

In a moment they had found it. It did double back to the right. Looking down it, they saw the faintest glimmer below. As their eyes had adjusted to the darkness, the way was readily apparent.

"Down to a light," 8 Manik repeated.

"What?" asked Naked Jaw.

"The old man," said 8 Manik.

The walls of the passage grew damp as they felt their way along. The air was rank and chill in the narrow stairway. After 21 steps, they found themselves in a narrow hallway. At the end, a door was half open. The light was brighter. There must be a torch in the room beyond. Silently they inched their way toward it. At the doorway, 8 Manik saw the back of Twin Rabbit. He was crouched, alert, like a jungle cat preparing to spring on its prey. Voices filtered through the opening as an old voice creaked unintelligible words. The withered tones of the chanting ground to a halt, and Twin Rabbit straightened, then stepped boldly into the room beyond. 8 Manik crept up to the door, crouched as Twin Rabbit had done, and peeked in.

Five stairs led down from the doorway to the stone floor. The walls on either side rose straight to the height of a man's shoulder, then angled together to form a steeply pitched roof with stone crossbeams wedged from one side to the other.

Painted on the walls was a procession of men and women, adorned with the headdresses of leadership. These were the images of the kings and two queens of Palenque, the line of descent that had ruled the city for hundreds of years and which claimed to stem from the gods themselves. When Pakal was laid to rest in this his tomb, these were the spirits who would come to guide him on his dangerous journey through the underworld.

In the center, an enormous slab, weighing perhaps five tons, was balanced on rollers. It nearly filled the room. The top was carved with a magnificent scene depicting Pakal at the moment of his death, falling into the waiting arms of the underworld. Underneath, 8 Manik guessed, must be the sarcophagus in which the ruler would be sealed when the lid was rolled forward and the rollers removed.

The oldest man that 8 Manik had ever seen was seated on the edge of the sarcophagus lid, looking with calm and impassive mien at the figure of Twin Rabbit. A white loincloth draped across his withered hips was the only clothing he wore. His chest, sagging with age, hung toward the paunch of his stomach. His face was a mass of wrinkles, with its hooked nose, sloping forehead, and lower lip drooping in elegant disdain. The eyes were half-lidded, but the pupils within gleamed with a curious intensity.

"Grandfather," said Twin Rabbit, "I have returned to claim what is my own."

"I am not surprised to see you." The voice quavered, but there was no sense of uncertainty in the tone.

"I knew that you would be here," gloated Twin Rabbit. "You thought that all your guards and cahals would protect you as they did that day when you drove me from your court. I knew that you would come to your tomb to renew your spiritual power. You thought you could extend your life for one more miserable year, but you didn't check the stars. Your red planet has been destroyed by my patron, the moon. Your days are finished."

"I knew you were coming," the old man's voice was unruffled. "A few days ago the body of a fowler was found in the Usamacinta. There was a great gash across the base of his neck, and in his mouth, the blade of an obsidian knife. The peasants who found him were amazed. They thought that perhaps one of the lords of the underworld had emerged to prey on men on the surface and came to me for protection. I knew it was a harbinger of your arrival."

"That's one of your old tricks," retorted Twin Rabbit. "Claiming to have foreknowledge of events might impress the headman of some village, but I know better."

"A cahal from Calakmul reported to me last night," continued the old man, "a most unusual encounter. He said he met a traveling noble whose men were shabbily arrayed and uncouth in their demeanor. The man claimed to come from the far south but knew nothing of the situation of his home city. His accent, while cultured, was that of a man of the north. He thought it strange. I knew you were on your way."

"And so you came here alone and unprotected, grandfather?" sneered Twin Rabbit.

"Chan Bahlum, your uncle and my heir, accompanied me. He brought his spear." The old man waved elegantly toward a corner of the room, which 8 Manik could not see.

"A man of fifty years. Having six toes will not help him. I can defeat both of you as easily as one."

"I am not alone," said Pakal. "As you see, my ancestors are all about me here. Without them I would have no right to be in this room."

"Paintings of men long dead," sneered Twin Rabbit.

"You, of all people, should know," the old man's voice for the first time beginning to be edged with contempt, "that the great lords do not dwell in the underworld as commoners do when they die. They survive the rigors of battle with the nine lords of death and are reborn on the surface of the world. They are renewed by what destroys lesser folk. In a truly great house, our ancestors become our descendants and companions as well."

Now it was Twin Rabbit's turn to let contempt enter his speech. "You speak of ancestors. These are not your ancestors; this is not your throne. You inherited the rulership of Palenque illegitimately, through a woman. Your father was a cahal, an underling." As he spoke, Twin Rabbit raised his spear and advanced toward the old man on the sarcophagus.

"And you would like to inherit the throne of Palenque from your mother as well," spat the old man, undaunted by the powerful physical presence and upraised spear of his grandson. "You think you could be ruler over north and south?"

"No! I will not inherit your throne. I will seize it. When I lay your heart on the altar in Tikal, the city will rally to me. I will return with a conquering army and make this place a permanent vassal state! What is mine by right I will take by force."

"You will never be able to escape," Pakal's voice remained as calm and self-assured as ever. "Already my return to the palace is delayed. Those who come looking for me will find you and exact a suitable revenge. The city lusts for war. Your heart on the altar would assure Chan Bahlum of an auspicious start to his reign."

"You are old and your men move slowly," said Twin Rabbit. "I'm not alone. There is a band that will help me cut my way out before the city can be mobilized. They are few, but they are bold and desperate. They know I will reward them well."

CHAPTER TWELVE

"I'm glad that you listened to my advice about mobilizing superior forces on the field of battle," said Pakal in a sardonic tone. "I thought you were dreaming the time away when I was talking to you. Now I see that you were giving an old man your attention, after all. You were right; the portents alone did not let me know of your arrival. Naked Jaw has brought you to me. And in return, he and his band will enjoy free passage in my lands, safe from punitive expeditions."

Naked Jaw stepped past 8 Manik through the doorway and into the crypt, lifting his spear and pointing it at Twin Rabbit's chest.

Twin Rabbit stared wildly between the two men, his eyes darting back and forth as if looking for some indication of how they had managed to deceive him so completely. Then he seemed to reset himself, looking not at Naked Jaw or Chan Bahlum, but at Pakal. His spear point wavered just inches from the old man's chest.

"Perhaps you have another ally?" asked Pakal, and 8 Manik realized that the old man had seen him crouching in the doorway. For a second, the eyes of Twin Rabbit and Chan Bahlum flickered toward him, then each snapped back, intent on his target. As he stepped into the room, it seemed that he was entering a room of statues: Pakal seated impassively on the huge slab of stone with Twin Rabbit's spear at his chest, Naked Jaw and Chan Bahlum, each on the alert, ready to attack the noble.

"Who is this? He doesn't look like a bandit to me." At first, 8 Manik thought that the question was addressed to Naked Jaw, but he realized that the lord was speaking to him directly.

"A market vendor, my lord," answered 8 Manik.

"And you have come to help this boy kill me?" Pakal used the verb that meant to slaughter an animal. "Is there much profit in that?" 8 Manik was surprised to hear such common speech from one so great.

"I have come because he has something that I value above all things," answered 8 Manik. "The life of my grandchild. If Twin Rabbit dies, my grandson will be killed. He may have killed him already, but I cannot take that chance."

"He's alive," blurted Twin Rabbit in desperation. "As long as I live, he will live."

"This child is dear to you." Pakal's voice was coolly indifferent. He was appraising the situation, assessing how much he would have to offer to gain 8 Manik's cooperation.

8 Manik looked at him with disdain. "He's as dear to me as my own son," he said. He had been about to say, "as dear to me as your son is to you" but it struck him that he had no way of knowing whether the lord's son was dear to him. Who knew what sentiments moved members of the noble caste? "In any case, what do I have to offer any of you?"

"You could run get my servants to help me," said Twin Rabbit. "One quick step and you are out of the room, out of reach. These men don't dare move, because I can take Pakal's life before they act. After I have dispatched Pakal, I can give you whatever you want."

"After you kill them, what would keep you from killing me?" asked 8 Manik. "Once I was free, I could tell your secrets. You would be insane to give me my grandson and let me go free."

Pakal laughed a mirthless cackle which made all of them flinch. "I would not like to trade in the market with this man," he said. "No wonder the traders of Tikal are renowned for their acumen.

"Now, listen to me, all of you," he went on. "Twin Rabbit does not dare kill me, because if he does, my son and Naked Jaw will slaughter him before he can get help. They do not dare to strike first against Twin Rabbit, because if they do, his lance will pierce my body before their action can take effect. If the merchant sides with us, he loses his son. If he sides with Twin Rabbit, he loses his life. It would appear that we are all trapped. What a wonderful world the gods have made! What a game they have set us to play, with our lives as the outcome."

He seemed to be enjoying the moment enormously. Perhaps, after years of dominating all within his sway, he was feeling the thrill of being in a situation in which the outcome was in doubt.

"No," said Naked Jaw to 8 Manik. "I know where your grandson is. Twin Rabbit sent his concubine to Seibal with the children. I had a man follow him into Tikal and he overheard their plans. Help us and I can take you to them. You know my men can travel more swiftly than any courier in the forest. We will arrive before the news of Twin Rabbit's death can possibly reach them and then we will rescue your grandchild."

"It's not true," snapped Twin Rabbit. "He's only just saying that to turn you against me. Go get my bodyguards and tell them to come. I'm the only one who can give you what you want. You may not trust me, but none of them offers any hope of saving the child. Do it for the good of Tikal. Pakal wants to make it a state enslaved to him. I want to shake off its bondage and make it the greatest city in the world."

"Be quiet," shouted 8 Manik. He could hear the echoes ringing up the stairwell. Rage boiled in him, overwhelming his fear and indecision with a rush, like a splinter of wood bursting into flame. "If I had the power, I'd shift this doorway and seal you all in. Then you could feed on one another!"

"You cannot go against the will of the gods," babbled Twin Rabbit, searching for anything that might move 8 Manik.

"The god of the merchants never sets below the horizon," said 8 Manik. "He is Ek Chuah, the north star, the constant guide, the Black Scorpion. He alone is always benevolent, always present. The rest of you slash and kill and plot against one another. You are not worthy to be leaders."

"And what does Ek Chuah, your constant guide, tell you that you must do?" asked Pakal. The aged voice was calm and sardonic. "Will you run and get Twin Rabbit's bodyguards to overwhelm us? Will you run and get Naked Jaw's men to overwhelm Twin Rabbit? It would appear that your constant guide is not of much use to you here, deep in the pyramid where one cannot see a star whether it sets or not. Better to have gods that demand sacrifice and guarantee success than one who merely guides from afar."

"I think each of you worships a sovereign deity that guides your actions," said 8 Manik. "You pursue glory and power for yourself and Palenque. Naked Jaw seeks freedom to take what he wants as he wills it. Twin Rabbit seeks domination over the whole world."

"And you?" Pakal's eyes were quizzical. "What is your constant guide? Profit? Pleasure? Ease?"

"The oldest and most powerful guide of all," said 8 Manik. "I seek to protect my offspring. That is the force that binds the bird to its nest and sends the jaguar to find its prey. There is another here who worships at the same altar."

"Who?" Pakal's voice was interested and surprised.

"You forget your own son, Chan Bahlam? What stops him from striking? If he manages to kill Twin Rabbit before you are stricken, he is a great son and worthy of the throne. If he fails and you are killed, the throne is his all the sooner. What keeps him from lashing out? He cannot lose."

"B-B-Because he is my father." The words came stumbling from Chan Bahlum's mouth. "He reigns in P-P-Palenque. It is my d-d-duty to help him."

"A good boy," said Pakal. His voice was stained with contempt for Chan Bahlum's straightforward loyalty. "But it does not matter. It is you who must choose."

"Too late," shouted Twin Rabbit in delight. "I hear footsteps on the stairs. My nagual has come to save me as the old man predicted!"

Involuntarily all of the men looked up, as if by staring through the walls of rock and mortar they could identify the figure approaching down the stairwell. In that moment, 8 Manik threw his body forward, knocking Pakal to one side. He felt the thrust of Twin Rabbit's spear across his shoulder blade, the tip just creasing his skin with a jagged slice of pain. In the hubbub, the torch on the wall careened wildly, then crashed to the floor, and the room was dark. 8 Manik found himself in a welter of thrashing arms and legs as everyone lashed out wildly.

8 Manik rolled to his left, struggling to reach the edge of the sarcophagus lid. Somewhere on the floor lay the shaft of the torch, the embers at the end still glowing. He wanted to drive the sharpened end into Twin Rabbit's body, to spear him like a fish. He felt Twin Rabbit catch him by the shoulder to pull him back. Powerless against the greater height and weight of his opponent, 8 Manik rolled onto his back and lashed out with his foot in the direction of Twin Rabbit's groin. In the darkness, the foot collided with Twin Rabbit's knee, bringing him crashing down on top of 8 Manik. He could feel the sacred dagger, still in its pouch, pressed between their bodies. Twin Rabbit's hands were around 8 Manik's throat, closing on his windpipe.

8 Manik's gripped the sacred dagger and pulled it, pouch and all from Twin Rabbit. Without taking it from its covering, he began smashing it into Twin Rabbit's side, hoping the point would slice through the material in the bag. The fingers tightened around 8 Manik's throat. He pounded with the knife again and again. Blood began gushing over his hands. He gripped tighter and jammed the knife into Twin Rabbit one more time. He was desperate for air, grappling to remain conscious. With a last, desperate thrust, he drove the dagger home, twisting the blade in the wound. The fingers around his neck loosened and a blissful rush of fresh air flooded into his lungs. He felt Twin Rabbit's body slump as the blood pulsed again and again over him.

Over his shoulder he saw light flicker in the doorway. Apparently the person who descended was carrying a torch. The rectangle grew brighter and a head peered cautiously through.

It was the face of Muan.

*   *   *   *   *

With an effort, Pakal pushed himself to a seated position on the slab. At his feet lay the body of Twin Rabbit, blood gushing from its wounds and guttering away through the gap between the sarcophagus lid and into the cavity below – the one intended to hold Pakal's body after death. To 8 Manik's amazement, the old face was creased with grief and silent tears poured over the wrinkled cheeks.

Muan put an arm around 8 Manik's waist and helped him to his feet. 8 Manik gripped his son, clutching his shoulders, unwilling to let go, as if any parting, no matter how brief would mean his child would be separated from him forever. Chan Bahlum and Naked Jaw stood silent, witnessing the wave of sorrow engulfing Pakal, shaking his delicate frame with enormous sobs. Finally, the paroxysm spent itself.

"He was my hope," Pakal gasped. "So big, so noble. He would have united the houses of Tikal and Palenque as the gods intended. No one could have stood against him. At my death, he would have reigned supreme. I was wrong to think he must serve as my vassal first. No soul so great can ever be an underling."

"He tried to kill you!" blurted 8 Manik. "He was a madman." Astounded by this turn of affairs he looked to Naked Jaw and Chan Bahlum for confirmation. Naked Jaw just shrugged. Chan Bahlum looked impassively on. Apparently, he had always lived with the sense that he didn't meet his father's expectations.

"We will bury him here, in my sarcophagus," announced Pakal. "He will wear the jade mask that has been prepared for me, bear the diadem of the god of rulership. In his right hand we will place a cube of jade, and in the left, the sphere. We will lower the lid upon him now, and when I die, the date of my death will be carved upon the lid. He will go to the underworld as a ruler of Palenque. Then the stairway will be filled so none can disturb him."

Slowly the old man let himself down off the sarcophagus lid and creaked toward the doorway. 8 Manik glared at him in contempt. At the portal, Pakal turned.

"He will need accompaniment through the underworld. He said he had men with him. You will sacrifice them to keep him company."

"He arrived with two men and a girl," answered Naked Jaw, the first to shake himself free from the astonishment of the event.

"Not enough. You will give of your men as well. That will make five, one for each point of the compass and one for the center. Leave them in the doorway, but make sure to provide room so that the sculptor can step past them when he comes to inscribe the date of my death."

He turned away. They could hear him wheezing as he made the laborious climb up the staircase.

"You're not going to do it?" said 8 Manik to Naked Jaw.

Naked Jaw shrugged. "Lose two of my men so the entire band can survive? It seems a good bargain to me."

"And the girl?"

"He slit her throat at the house before we left. He said it would ensure success."

"You are repellant," said 8 Manik.

"Not so bad as you might think," said Naked Jaw. "When men join my band they know that death is our constant companion."

"But to kill your own men? That makes you no better than…"

"An outlaw?" said Naked Jaw, quizzically.

"I was going to say, a great lord," said 8 Manik.

Naked Jaw bent over the body of Twin Rabbit and pulled the ceremonial dagger of Stormy Sky from the wound. "He always said that this proved he was the son of Shield Skull. It might prove useful. Tikal is a great city. It needs a great leader."

"You are as insane as he was," said 8 Manik. "The cahals will never accept someone like you as a leader."

"The cahals will accept anyone who makes them rich and powerful," said Naked Jaw. "Of course, I don't know much about how people in Tikal behave. You could teach me, and I will restore your grandson to you."

"I will teach you after you restore my grandson," said 8 Manik. "I've had enough of the honor of kings."

Naked Jaw laughed and started up the stairway. 8 Manik looked at Muan.

"If you had not come at the moment you did," he said. "We could all be dead, little Hunapu included."

"I followed you as best I could, but I got lost in the darkness. Finally, I decided to go to the central plaza. When I saw light in the temple, I climbed up, took the torch and came down the stairway."

"So," said 8 Manik. "Everything may be as it once was."

He looked up as he climbed the stairway. When it turned, he could see a rectangle of lighter gray in the entry above. The first rays of dawn were beginning to illuminate the world.

AUTHORS NOTE

Pakal lived two years more and died in his eightieth year, a remarkable age for the time. When he left for his journey into the underworld, he had reigned since his mother passed the kingship to him at the age of twelve. Chan Bahlum succeeded his father and completed the massive three-pyramid center, which replicated, on earth, the three supports of the first fireplace in creation. They are known to tourists as the Temple of the Cross, the Temple of the Foliated Cross, and the Temple of the Sun.

Palenque reached the zenith of its power under Pakal and his two sons. Pakal's second son, Kan Xul II, expanded the realm to its greatest extent. In the ninth year of his reign, he led a raid into the territory of neighboring Tonina but was captured and held prisoner for nine more years before he was sacrificed. In the ensuing political chaos, cities under the sway of Palenque broke free. Attempts to restore its glory were only intermittently successful and after 800 CE all record of the dynasty disappears.

In 682 Tikal experienced a resurgence under its 26th ruler, known as Jasaw Chan Ka'wil, "the heavenly standard bearer." This energetic ruler reestablished patterns of religious architecture dormant for two hundred years, excavating and burying stelae celebrating the accomplishments of Tikal's greatest ruler, Stormy Sky, three centuries earlier. After a hundred years of humiliation, this leader, who claimed to be the reincarnation of Stormy Sky, enabled Tikal to become again the strongest power of the Mayan states and the largest city ever created by the Maya.

In 1949, a Mexican archaeologist, Alberto Ruiz, discovered a stairway leading down inside the Temple of the Inscriptions which had been completely filled in at the time of Pakal's death. Years of careful excavation brought him to the crypt, which contained the skeletons of four men and one woman. On November 27, 1952 he managed to raise the five-ton sarcophagus lid, which clearly identified the inhabitant of the tomb as Pakal. Inside were human remains richly endowed with grave goods.

Physical anthropologists studying these remains, however, have concluded that the man buried in the sarcophagus could have reached an age of no more than 40 years at the time of his death.